Three Tempting Tales of Lord Larry

Three Tempting Tales
of
Lord Larry

A Trio of Regency Short Romances

Susan Gee Heino

ISBN: 978-0-9886175-8-2

Contents

The Delicate Plot to Bury Lord Larry

A Regency Short Story

by Susan Gee Heino

Dedication

To Jack.
Thanks for letting me plot to my little heart's content.

Chapter 1

London, England, May, 1817

Netta Maitland crept through the darkness, her soft slippers padding silently over the dirty cobblestone. She shouldn't be here, of course, but that was the whole point. No one would ever imagine that she'd come here of her own free will. She could claim Larry had done all sorts of dreadful things to her before... before the horrible tragedy that was just about to befall him.

After tonight, no one would ever want to marry her and she could be free to live her life. Alone. Which would be infinitely better than married to someone she didn't love.

At least, she hoped that would be the case. Right now she was beginning to doubt the wisdom of this scheme. Did she truly want to go through with this?

She wrinkled her nose. The smell of rotting fish and other disgusting aromas filled the air. The docks were not a fit place for a lady at all, and of course this was entirely the point. She stepped around a greasy puddle and shuddered as some sort of small creature rustled in a trash heap nearby. Larry had better show up soon or she might just lose her will and go rushing home like a coward.

"Psst, Netta! Over here."

She heard him hiss her name from behind an assortment of grimy crates. Good. Just as they had planned, so far.

"I really don't like being here," she whispered, scurrying to him. "Is everything set the way it should be?"

His eyes were dark, but his determination shone

1

through in the moonlight. He was far too much like a brother for her to consider whether or not his features might be considered attractive, but she certainly did admire his conviction. Not simply any man might have come up with this plot, and certainly few of them would be willing to carry it out.

"It is," he assured her. "You're certain that Mrs. Plunket will be here on time, with your father?"

"She will. I've sold my mother's necklace to pay my maid to tell everyone that you've absconded with me, and I've begged Mrs. Plunket to go along with our plan. She has promised to bring Papa charging after us. But... are you positive this is what you want?"

He did not even hesitate before he replied. "It is. This is the only way for us, Netta. Our families will never let us be happy unless we do this."

"But death is so very final. Is there truly no other way?"

"I'm sorry, but no. I'm afraid after tonight, you and I will not be likely to see each other again."

Oh, but she hated those words. What would she do without Larry? They'd grown up together; he was the one she shared all her secrets with. Most of them, at any rate. Now after this she'd have one monster of a secret to carry, and she'd bear it alone.

But he was right. The best way out of their current predicament was for Larry to die. She cared for him deeply, so she'd do her part to help him along.

"Very well, then. What do I do?"

He reached into his coat and pulled out a pistol. It was a dreadful looking thing, huge and cumbersome. And deadly.

"As soon as we see our people arrive, you must pretend to fear me."

"I certainly fear *that* thing."

"Excellent. I will use it to threaten you, and you will

2

fight. Your father, of course, will be furious and wish to save you, so you will run to him and I will run down this pier and get into that boat."

"It's not a very big boat. How are you supposed to get away from Papa?"

"I will shoot myself, of course."

Just the sound of it made her cringe. "Not really, you won't."

"No. Not really. I will have powder in the pan, but no ball. It will flash and I will pretend to be shot. Your father will still be here with you, and from this distance he will only see me fall and think I have died."

"And then? They will expect to come find your body, of course."

"But they will never find one. Once I have died aboard that boat, I will be out of sight. That will allow me to ignite the gunpowder I have hidden on board. While you are here, keeping your father distracted with your hysterics, he will not see me slip into the water and swim under the pier. The boat will then burst into flame and eventually crumble into the water. Everyone will assume my body is lost."

"And by then you will be gone."

"Yes. I have to go away, Netta. It's a good plan, and it will work. Are you up for this?"

She drew a deep breath and tried not to think of anything beyond what she must do now, in this moment. "Yes. It is for the good of both of us, Larry."

"That's my girl."

"Just please, promise when you are safe somewhere you will write me. Use any name you wish in your letters—I will read them and respond, I promise. I will always want to know you are safe, and that you've found what you are searching for."

"I will. And don't worry, you know that I... wait, listen. Is that a carriage?"

3

It was. She was suddenly shaking, trembling as if she truly was terrorized and fearing for her life. Mrs. Plunket was right on schedule, bringing Papa to catch them here and to play his unwitting part in their outrageous scheme. She steeled herself for her performance.

"Good luck," Larry whispered as he raised his gun to her neck and dragged her out from behind the crates.

His performance was convincing, and there was no doubt hers would be, too. The chattering of her teeth and the tears welling in her eyes were very real indeed.

But it was not Papa's carriage that clattered to a stop before them. Larry swore audibly as they both made out the familiar crest emblazoned on the door.

"Lord Gladbourne!" she breathed.

"Damn it all. How did he find us here?"

"We aren't prepared for this, Larry," she spoke through clenched teeth.

"Stay with the plan," he mumbled. "We can still do this, Netta. Don't waver."

But this was Lord Gladbourne! How on earth could she not waver? The man made her head spin and her knees turn to jelly. She couldn't do this... they had to change their plan. Fooling her near-sighted, half-drunk Papa was one thing, but Lord Gladbourne? He'd see through them in a heartbeat.

The carriage door flung open and the man leapt out, his black capes flying and his wintery gray eyes flashing with fury. Every muscle in his six foot frame seemed tight, wound like a spring and ready to trigger. He stalked toward them, his boots ringing on the cold, damp stones.

"Stay back, cousin!" Larry ordered. "I brought her here to end her, and I don't mind having an audience."

"Good God, Larry. Put the pistol down and let her go," Lord Gladbourne demanded.

4

"I told you I wasn't interested in matrimony," Larry called, pressing the gun into Netta's skin. "But you and that greedy father of hers don't care what I want, do you? Well, it's easy enough to be rid of her. And I'll do it if you take one step more."

Gladbourne's eyes still blazed, but he stopped in his tracks. The driver atop his carriage shifted as if to climb down to assist, but his lordship held up a hand to stay him. Clearly he was taking Larry's threat seriously. Could he really be so very concerned for her safety? The idea of it made Netta want to grin like a simpleton.

But she couldn't. She had to keep pretending to fear Larry. She batted her eyes and gave a pitiful whimper. Inside she was dancing a jig, though.

"Let her go," Lord Gladbourne ordered again.

Larry's repeated refusal went unheard as the sound of another carriage racing toward them interrupted. In no time at all, Papa's carriage appeared around a near corner, his horses pushed hard and the carriage swaying precariously. Ah, so now their plan was in full play. Larry had been correct, after all. Even with Lord Gladbourne's unexpected arrival, perhaps they could make this happen.

*   *   *

Gladbourne forced himself to keep still. He wanted to rush his cousin, to grab the unhinged bastard by the throat and choke him until he dropped that damn pistol and Miss Maitland was safe. Then he wanted to grab her and hold her so that nothing like this could ever happen again.

He could not do either of those things, however. As long as Larry held that weapon, there wasn't much Gladbourne could do. Never in a hundred years would he risk Netta's life by acting in anger.

Her father, on the other hand, seemed not to have any of those hesitations. His carriage rolled to a stop and Mr.

Maitland came tumbling out. As usual, it was clear the older man was well into his cups. How he had produced such a temperate, virtuous daughter, Gladbourne had no idea. Mr. Harry Maitland was a whiskey-soaked tosspot and he was not deserving of such an offspring. Not that Gladbourne had any intention of letting his lunatic cousin deprive the man of her, deserving or not.

"What the devil is going on here?" Maitland bellowed.

"He says he'll kill me, Papa!" Netta called out to her father. She did appear fully terrified, yet Gladbourne credited her for keeping her head. Her voice sounded remarkably solid and she had not swooned dead away as some lesser female might have.

"He'd better not kill you," Maitland rumbled. " If he does, then I'll sure as hell kill him."

And a fat lot that would do for the poor girl. Obviously it would be up to Gladbourne to diffuse the situation here. He still found it incredible that his cousin would do such a thing. Hold a pistol to Netta and threaten murder? Hell, Larry loved Netta, he always had. The two were as kindred souls since all the way back to their childhood. What on earth could have come over the man to suddenly cause him to react this way?

"You don't want to hurt her, Larry," Gladbourne said calmly. "Let me help you. Put down your pistol and—"

"And I'll blast his fool heart out with mine!" Maitland announced, producing his own heavy pistol and waving it in Larry's direction.

Unfortunately that meant it was also in Netta's direction. Hellfire, the poor woman was just as likely to be shot by her own ruddy father as she was by her brain-addled fiancé! Gladbourne had to do something fast.

"Listen to me, Larry," he said, daring to inch one single step closer. "You don't want to do this. You're hurting her;

please let her go."

He met his cousin's wild eyes. Moonlight splashed over his face, reflected off the dirty water that lapped at the wharf. Gladbourne could see cold, dark resolve behind Larry's eyes. Whatever would come to pass due to this chain of events, Larry was entirely committed to it. He was not, however, going to kill Netta. Gladbourne knew that as surely as he knew his own name.

He breathed a sigh of relief.

It was short lived, though. He watched his cousin whisper something into Netta's ear, then without warning she was thrust violently from him. She screamed. Gladbourne lunged forward to catch her before she tumbled to the filthy ground.

Larry darted away, leaping over the low wall that edged the wharf and landing with a thud on the wooden pier just a few feet below. Gladbourne scooped Netta into his arms and pulled her tight against him, twisting his body to keep her sheltered from both sets of gentlemen with weapons. Larry was rushing down the length of the pier, toward a small boat that was moored at the end, partially obstructed from view.

"I'll shoot the bastard!" Mr. Maitland shouted, taking aim.

"No!" Netta cried suddenly, breaking free from Gladbourne and running toward her father.

Gladbourne swore. Would she risk her life for his damned cousin even now, after how abominably he'd treated her? He let Larry make his feeble attempt at escape and hurried after Netta, pulling her out of the line of her father's fire.

"Don't shoot him, Papa," she begged. "He needs our help. He says he's going to kill himself!"

"I'm happy to help him with that!"

Gladbourne had reached Maitland now and put his hand

out to avert the man's weapon. Whether or not Larry deserved to be shot was a bit of a moot point, but the earl was not about to let it happen.

"I think your daughter has suffered enough for one night," he announced. "Let's not add to her horror by shooting her fiancé before her very eyes."

"She's welcome to go wait in the carriage, then," Maitland growled, shoving Gladbourne away.

"Damn it, be careful, man. Have you no concern at all for your own daughter?"

He made sure to put himself between Netta and her blustering, foolhardy father. But she had eyes only for Larry.

"Look, he's getting into that boat!" she said, pointing.

And so he was. What the devil was the man doing, planning to row himself all the way out to the channel? Gladbourne would see that Miss Maitland was taken to safety then he'd get someone after Larry. The poor sap really did need help for whatever had come over him.

But Larry wasn't rowing, or shoving the boat away from the pier in a misguided attempt to escape. He stood in it, his head barely visible over the edge of the pier. Gladbourne had a clear enough view of him, though, to clearly make out the pistol held up toward his temple.

"I won't give you the satisfaction of shooting me, Maitland!" Larry yelled toward them. "I'll do it for you!"

Without any further warning Larry's pistol rang out. The calm of the deserted docks was shattered by the horrible sound. Miss Maitland shrieked as Larry's body crumpled down into the boat, hidden behind the pier. Gladbourne gaped in shock.

The fool had actually done it! By God, his cousin had shot himself. Miss Maitland fell against her father, weeping.

They all stood there, frozen, for a moment or two. At last Gladbourne shook himself back to reality. He started toward the pier.

"I'll go see if there can be anything done for him."

"No!" Miss Maitland cried. She sounded desperate, and dashed after him to grab at his sleeve. "No... you can't go out there. I... I think I'm going to faint."

For half a second he was confused, then her lovely eyes rolled shut and he could see her body going limp. He reached to catch her just in time. She sagged into his arms and he held her securely. The poor thing, as if being abducted and threatened at gunpoint wasn't enough. Now she'd had to watch her beloved take his own life in such a gruesome way? Gladbourne's heart broke for her.

"Good heavens, did that young man just shoot himself?"

The voice came from Maitland's carriage. Gladbourne glanced over to see Miss Maitland's woefully drab companion, Mrs. Plunket, emerging wide-eyed from its interior. She was pale and waved a black handkerchief in front of her nose.

"The damn coward saved me a lead ball. Left my daughter with no fiancé, though," Mr. Maitland railed.

Miss Maitland moaned softly. Gladbourne tried not to pay too much attention to her supple curves pressed up against him. This was clearly not the right time to be so very aware of his persistent attraction to the woman. She needed much more than that from him just now. He patted her gently and brushed a strand of her dark, silky hair away from her porcelain cheek.

"There now, you've had quite the shock," he murmured. "But Mrs. Plunket is here. She can take you back to your home."

She stirred just slightly in his arms, so he touched her cheek again. It was as soft and as perfect as he'd ever

9

imagined. Slowly her bright, blue eyes opened.

"But Larry is..."

"Shh, I will tend to him. You should go with Mrs. Plucket now. Your father will see you both safely home."

Her ivory brow furrowed and she glanced past him, out toward the end of the pier. She seemed to be unsure what had happened, as if her brain simply couldn't comprehend what her eyes had clearly seen.

"I don't understand it," she murmured. "Why didn't he..."

Her voice trailed away and Gladbourne would have given up his title and estate to have known what to tell her just now.

The uncomfortable silence was broken again, this time by a sudden explosion. Miss Maitland's trembling body jolted and Gladbourne was shaken by a wave of heat and charred bits of debris. The boat had suddenly combusted! There must have been gunpowder aboard and a spark from Larry's pistol must have ignited it. Damn it, but if Larry had not been fully dispatched by his own efforts, this would have surely done the trick now.

Mrs. Plunket screeched. "He blew up a gun boat!"

"Impetuous fool!" Mr. Maitland cried.

The young lady simply buried her face against Gladbourne's chest. He held her tightly, comforting her as best as he could. He could feel her slight body wracked with the first pitiful sobs. No doubt she'd suffer through many of them now, thanks to his damned, cold-hearted cousin.

"I'll never see him again," she said quietly.

Her words were muffled against Gladbourne's coat, but he heard them. He knew what they meant, too. She still loved Larry with all of her heart and would spend the rest of her life grieving him. He knew he'd be grieving, too, and

10

could only hope she would believe it was for the loss of his cousin.

Susan Gee Heino

Chapter 2

Netta let herself be taken home, happy that after all the emotion at the docks neither Papa nor Mrs. Plunket seemed in any mood for conversation. She would not have been capable of it even if they had. Larry was gone. She'd never see him again; the fact that he'd completed their plan and been able to make the boat explode was proof of that. He was off to pursue his dream and no one could stand in his way.

Her head was a jumble of thoughts and emotions, and she wished she could tell herself they were all because of Larry. They were not. Her heart pounded erratically, she felt dizzy and strange, tears streamed down her face but at the same time she wanted to sing to the skies. Oh, what a mess she was now! And it was not due to Larry.

It was Lord Gladbourne. Heavens, but he'd held her in his strong arms and patted her gently, almost as if he cared for her! It had been wonderful. She should have made herself swoon on him ages ago.

Except that she knew, of course, he did not care for her. He'd been the one most eager to see her wed Larry. He and Papa had planned every last detail of the upcoming marriage, forcing Larry to go along with their plans. But now, due to her efforts, poor Lord Gladbourne would spend the rest of his life thinking he'd witnessed his cousin's death and been helpless to stop it. All Netta could do at that time was whimper like a helpless child. Indeed, Gladbourne would never think of her as anything but a part of that sad situation and she doubted she'd ever quite forgive herself.

"I'll help you get to bed, dearie," Mrs. Plunket said as they shuffled up the stairway toward Netta's bedroom at the

13

rear of their narrow townhouse. "You've had a trying time of it, to be sure."

"I can't believe he's gone now," she mumbled, letting the older woman help her out of her gown once they were inside.

"But you said it wouldn't be real. Mr. Garville was only pretending to blow himself up." Mrs. Plunket paused, wrinkling her brow in confusion and concern.

"Yes, but the whole point of this is so that he might find the woman he loves and carry her away before her father forces her to marry another. They will likely have to run all the way to America, and I am very sad that I'll never see him again."

"Pity you didn't simply marry him yourself then."

"I don't want to marry him for myself! Please, Mrs. Plunket, we mustn't discuss this. What if Papa were to hear? It's important that everyone sees me grieving his loss and that we never speak of this again."

"Very well, my dear. I must say, though, that it seems an awful lot of effort just to get out of marriage."

"That's because an awful lot of effort was being put into getting us married," Netta muttered. "But now we are free of those plans."

Mrs. Plunket sniffed bitterly. "Well, he is, at least. You're the unfortunate jilt of an unstable man who just blew his brains out and exploded a boat. Don't be surprised if you bear the stain of that for a while. Let's just hope that when you do find a man you might wish to marry, the taint has worn off from all this. Heaven forbid that you might end up permanently ruined after tonight."

These thoughts hadn't escaped Netta's attention. Indeed, she would likely be an object of pity for some time to come, and surely there would be whispers and innuendo. Her lengthy friendship with Larry had always given people reason to talk, and now this would no doubt seal society's perceptions. What exactly *had* been her relationship with Lord Larry over all these years? Would she be fit for another after this? She'd certainly done herself no favors by helping Larry this way.

Not that it mattered very much. So what if no decent man thought her worthy of notice after this? She'd never noticed any of them—no one beyond Gladbourne. Unfortunately, he'd never noticed her. Not in the way she had longed to be noticed.

The more time she spent in Lord Gladbourne's presence over the years, the more he had pulled back and left Larry to interact with her. This past year that she and Larry had been officially engaged, his lordship had been positively scarce. The few times they had run across him at some public function, he'd merely been polite, asking after their wedding plans and making it clear that the sooner they were wed the happier he'd be. As head of the family, he seemed to take Larry's matrimonial state as his personal responsibility and clearly wanted to have things wrapped up neatly as soon as possible. Netta supposed Gladbourne would not have to dip into the family coffers to support Larry so very often if he had her dowry to keep him.

Why on earth had Gladbourne been the one to capture her heart? Why, after these recent years of his coldness and indifference, did she still see him as the charming, compassionate young man who made her laugh and taught her how to fish in the stream on his father's estate? A more sensible woman would have purged him from her mind by now, forgot girlish infatuation and set her sights on someone more attainable, someone who might actually care for her in return.

But no. Mrs. Plunket pulled the covers up as Netta slid into her bed, and she knew it would be another sleepless night, longing for Gladbourne and knowing she was the biggest fool on the planet. Even the great loss of her best friend tonight was not enough to turn her thoughts from the way she had felt in Gladbourne's arms.

Those heavenly moments would have to last her a lifetime.

"Rest now," Mrs. Plunket said as she put out the candles. "I'll let the servants know to leave you to sleep in the morning. Who knows if Lord Gladbourne will involve magistrates in this matter or if you'll be asked to give testimony for any of this, but surely for the next day or two we can turn away any callers. After that, we'll just have to see where things stand. I certainly hope I didn't do the wrong thing by helping with this charade."

"You didn't, Mrs. Plunket. Thank you. I can't tell you how much I appreciate your help and knowing I can count on your discretion."

The lady sniffed again, but the hint of concern and warmth in her eyes reassured Netta. The older woman would honor their arrangement.

"Good night, dear Netta. We'll just see what tomorrow holds."

*   *   *

Lord Gladbourne paced the length of Mr. Maitland's drawing room and swore silently at himself. He was quaking inside like some sort of schoolboy. Why should he be such a sap this morning? He'd come specifically to speak with the gentleman, not the daughter. He asked after her, of course, merely to be polite, and was not really surprised to be told she was indisposed at the moment. Not at all surprising, considering what she'd been through the night before. Miss Maitland would not be joining them today. He should have no reason to be jittery and nervous.

Yet he was.

"So his body hasn't been found," Mr. Maitland asked slowly, his voice still thick from what had, no doubt, been a very long light with a very large amount of whiskey.

"No, sir. It has not."

"Then the magistrate considers he might still be... alive?"

"No, sir. I'm afraid the consensus is that he could not have survived the gunshot, and even if he did, the subsequent explosion and fire would have finished him off. He likely burned with the boat, then went to the bottom of the Thames with it."

It was a cold, horrible way to describe his cousin's demise. The words felt jagged on his lips as he spoke them. Yet, there were no other words he could use. Whatever had come over Larry in those last hours, the poor soul had been driven to do horrible things. There was simply no way to embellish the truth.

Mr. Maitland shook his gray head. "Netta will not like to hear of it, though I daresay she knew this would be the report."

"I cannot tell you how sorry I am for all that my cousin has put her through."

"Indeed. To be dragged into such a thing... the gossips will wag their tongues off. I suppose there is nothing for us to do but retreat to the country. My sister will have us, I hope. My poor girl can eat her heart out there, away from the scandal of ruin."

"Ruin?"

"Well, you don't think society will ever let her forget what happened to her, do you? No, she'll likely be turned away from polite society after this."

"But she's done nothing wrong. Surely your friends would never hold her accountable for my cousin's erratic behavior."

"Mrs. Plunket informs me rumors are already flying,"

Mr. Maitland said, tsking lowly. "I'm afraid there's little hope of salvaging Netta's reputation. Suicide leaves quite the dark blot, my lord."

"You can't mean she will be forced to bear his disgrace all her life?"

"And people are bound to learn of the fact that your cousin lured her out of our house in the middle of the night. What sort of lady does that? No, she's ruined for sure."

"It can't be as bad as all that."

"I fear that it is. I'm not a wealthy man, and we don't have the connections to make people overlook this sort of thing. My daughter was lucky to have maternal grandparents who could provide a hefty dowry—that's how she snagged your fine cousin, after all. But now it's unlikely any other decent man will have her."

The sudden thought raced through Gladbourne's mind like a wildfire. He didn't even try to slow it down, to give common sense a moment to catch up. Words were already forming so he blurted them out.

"I'll have her."

"Er, what was that?"

"It makes perfect sense. My cousin disappointed Miss Maitland. He betrayed her and cast her into scandal, breaking her heart."

"Yes, but... did you say...?"

"I did, yes. If you'll allow it, sir, I'll marry your daughter. It's the least I can do to make up for my cousin's behavior."

"Let me make sure I understand you," Mr. Maitland said slowly. "You're offering for Netta? You would marry her and make her your countess and see that she is protected from scandal and ruin?"

"Indeed, sir," Gladbourne replied. "If she would be inclined to accept the offer, of course."

"By God, I assure you she'll be inclined. I'll personally see to it!"

Gladbourne found himself struggling between two instincts. On one hand, he felt suddenly as if he could leap up onto Mr. Maitland's faded settee and shout "Huzzah!" On the other hand, he felt as if he should rush out of the room and book passage on a ship bound for Australia. What in God's name had he just done?

He'd offered to marry Miss Maitland. What could he be thinking? She did not want to marry him. She barely seemed to tolerate being in the same room with him lately. Worse, she'd just seen the man she did wish to marry die a horrible death. How on earth could he even consider insulting the woman by proposing to her while poor Larry had not even been gone twenty-four hours?

But he had offered for her and it did make perfect sense. Larry was his cousin, after all. He felt a certain responsibility after what had happened. He was doing the girl a favor by offering her marriage. Her father was pleased enough with the notion. Surely once Miss Maitland understood how dire her situation was she'd be happy to consider Gladbourne's offer. She might even be grateful.

He'd suggest to her father that they allow her a few days to recover from her ordeal before he made his proposal to her. It would give her nerves time to settle. With luck, it might give his nerves time to settle, too. He would most certainly need some time to gather his courage before facing Miss Maitland with a proposal. Right now he suddenly felt as if he might vomit.

He choked just a bit when he heard her voice from the doorway.

"What will I be inclined for, Papa? What are you and Lord Gladbourne discussing?"

Apparently Mr. Maitland did not have the common courtesy to be sensitive of the young lady's fragile nervous condition. Or Gladbourne's. He answered her quite frankly.

"You will be inclined to accept Lord Gladbourne's offer of marriage."

The lady's eyes went huge and round. She glanced from her father to Gladbourne, the incredulity obvious. Clearly she was appalled that he would do such a thing, bring up such a tender topic when her loss was so raw. She must think him the worst sort of boor and opportunist.

"It is simply to protect you from the scandal and gossip that will surely come after what my cousin has done," he said quickly, although her expression did nothing to convince him she understood. He charged forward in his awkward explanation. "I feel it is nothing more than my duty to stand up where Larry has fallen down in your regard. My cousin robbed you of a groom, so I offer a replacement. I know neither of us prefers this situation, but I think it will be for the best. Please consider my offer, Miss Maitland."

There. He'd made it as convenient as possible, avoiding any sign of sentiment or emotion. It was entirely up to her to decide what to do now. He steeled himself for her instant refusal.

But he was spared. She blinked—still wide-eyed—and replied.

"Very well, sir. I accept."

Chapter 3

Netta had been engaged to Lord Gladbourne for more than a month now. Four weeks, six days, and eleven hours. Not that she intended to be counting.

Of course she was counting, though. She counted every moment since the man had appeared in her drawing room the day after Larry's disappearance and made his cold, sensible plea. The only moments during these past weeks that had not dragged on in infinite frustration were the two and a half hours that she had actually spent in his lordship's presence.

Two and a half hours. She would have only one more to add onto that when she finally stood before the minister to marry the man! How could she possibly go through with this?

Indeed, she had no hesitation for herself. She had accepted his proposal without giving it a second thought. It was a dream come true for her! Except that in her dream, the gentleman would actually be in love with her, not simply acting out of some misplaced sense of duty.

She was a horrible person to allow him to attach himself to her on these conditions. If she had any Christian charity in her soul, she would take the opportunity of this ball Papa was giving them to set poor Gladbourne free. He certainly had made it clear this wedding they had planned for tomorrow was a matter of obligation, not desire. He would be marrying her out of some tragic sense of guilt, not for any of the reasons she longed for.

Why hadn't she told him no? She should have. He merited as much from her. Surely there would be a special torment visited on her in the afterlife for first deceiving the man about his cousin's death, then accepting his marriage proposal. She was a weak-willed, selfish liar. He deserved so much better.

But heavens, to become his wife tomorrow! To think that she might have a whole lifetime to win him over, to make him care for her just a bit. That fantasy was too tempting to let go.

She would, though. Tonight. It was her last chance to do the right thing for him and confess all. No doubt he would hate her for it, but she couldn't live with herself if she did not. After tonight's ball, the man could go on with his life and perhaps eventually find the happiness he deserved.

She scowled, glancing over the crowd in their rented rooms and noticed that Gladbourne did, indeed, seem happy at the moment. He was conversing quite fluently with Miss Amelie D'Arnaud. The young lady trilled with laughter and playfully fluttered her lashes while she spoke in hushed tones. Gladbourne was smiling more than Netta had ever seen him smile at any of her conversation.

The nerve of that ridiculous French tart, shamelessly flirting when everyone knew Gladbourne was to be married. Just for that, Netta had half a mind *not* to break their engagement.

But then again, how much worse would her misery be if the man flirting with Miss D'Arnaud was not simply her fiancé, but her *husband*? She could not go through with the wedding. He did not want her, and she couldn't bear the shame and the loneliness of being his unwanted wife. Better to just bear the loneliness.

She began making her way toward him. It was sheer agony to greet friends and neighbors as she moved through the room, everyone wishing her happy and assuming her rosy cheeks and glistening eyes were from joy. It would surely come as a shock to all of them when no wedding actually occurred.

She was near to Gladbourne now and his eyes caught on hers. His smile dimmed and her heart broke just a little bit more. There were a few things on Miss D'Arnaud she wouldn't mind breaking, as well.

"And here is my intended," he said, raising his voice from the softer tones he had been using with his fluttering companion. "Miss Maitland, may I present Miss Amelie D'Arnaud?"

She nodded and pretended to have no latent animosity toward the lady. "How nice to meet you."

It was wholly objectionable, but she had to admit Miss Amelie was even more beautiful up close than she had been from across the room. Netta knew who she was—the most celebrated of this season's debutantes—but she'd never had opportunity for introduction. She wished she could still say that.

"Miss D'Arnaud 's mother is a good friend of my mother," Gladbourned explained. "They have spent the past years on the continent but now have returned to London."

Netta bit her cheeks as she smiled. "How lovely. You must have fascinating stories to tell."

"I am certainly not fascinating," Miss D'Arnaud said in her disgustingly cultured accent. "But his lordship is making me feel as if I am not entirely dull."

"I'm sure that he is," Netta said, feeling her left eye twitch just a bit. "I've heard others say that he is an excellent conversationalist."

Hopefully conversation was the only fascinating thing he'd been doing with Miss D'Arnaud. Not that it ought to be Netta's business, of course. She was going to release him from their arrangement, after all. But still...

"I think in his conversation your fiancé is a bit single-minded," Miss D'Arnaud said with a pretty pink pout and flashing eyes. "But I suppose that is to be expected in him, no?"

No. Most definitely no. It didn't take much effort to determine what single topic would be in the forefront of his mind as he conversed with Miss D'Arnaud. Netta would prefer not to know anything about it.

Obviously Lord Gladbourne felt the same way. He interrupted Miss D'Arnaud in mid fascination.

"Will you excuse us, Miss D'Arnaud? I see that the dancers are taking their place and I promised a waltz to Miss Maitland."

This declaration caught Netta off guard. He had most certainly *not* promised her a waltz, or any other dance. She would remember if he had. Was this simply some excuse to get her away from Miss D'Arnaud so she would not notice his obvious interest in the girl, or was he actually planning to dance with her? She could scarcely let herself wonder.

"I'm sure you never did promise a dance, sir," she said quietly when they were safely away from Miss D'Arnaud. "If you would rather not, I will not mind."

He frowned. Now she had upset him.

"Don't you think it would appear odd to our guests if the happy couple did not partake in at least one dance at a ball given in our honor?" he asked.

But of course, she should have realized this would be his reason. It was his whole reason for asking her to marry him, after all. He was very concerned with what people would think, what they might whisper, and how he was upholding his duty at any given moment. Very well, then. She had no wish to embarrass him or give anyone reason to think ill of him.

"We certainly wouldn't wish to appear odd, would we?" she said, brushing her heartache aside. "I'll waltz with you, then. But I must warn you of one thing, though."

"What is that?"

"For appearances sake, you might wish you had not asked. I am a terrible dancer, my lord."

For the first time in what must have been a year or more, she met his eyes and found him actually smiling. *At her!* Her heartache was gone as the suddenly-vibrant organ tumbled over itself and pounded inside her chest as if the dance were over instead of just beginning. Lord Gladbourne was smiling at her and imaginary angel choirs burst into song overhead. He took her hand and led her into position, holding her by the waist and pulling her close.

"Perhaps, Miss Maitland, you've simply lacked the proper partner."

*　　*　　*

God, but he had missed her these past weeks, forcing himself to avoid her and allow her to grieve Larry in peace. The funeral had been a small, private affair and Miss Maitland's sorrow had been crushing. She'd barely been able to look at Gladbourne. It was obvious she was not going into this marriage out of any great wish for it.

But damn it, Larry was gone and he had never been worthy of her. Gladbourne was sorry for the way things had gone, but he would not be sorry for stepping up and offering Netta a better life than she would have had otherwise. He just wished she would not be so dashed distant and cold toward him.

He had to be patient, though. She'd been through so much and simply needed more time. He would tread lightly, not press her, and let the wounds caused by his cousin heal at their own pace. Someday Netta would look beyond the empty place Larry had left in her heart. He would be there for her then and he would find a way to make her love him.

For now, though, holding her in his arms as they danced

was blissful torment. He knew she would have refused this waltz if she could have, and he felt just the slight sting of guilt for practically forcing her into it. Only slight, though. Her warmth and the scent of her hair made his moral dilemma easier to ignore. Plus, despite what she had said, she was a delightful dancing partner.

"You lied to me, my dear," he said after several moments of whirling silence between them.

She must have been lost in thought because suddenly she jolted. "What? Er, what do you mean, sir?"

"About dancing," he said, wishing he'd have caught her beautiful eyes for more than just a passing glance before she looked away again. "You told me you weren't very good at it."

Her cheeks colored. "As you can see, I was being perfectly honest about that. My dancing skills have been hopelessly neglected, I'm afraid."

"Neglect is something you should never have to endure, Miss Maitland. I will be very happy to see that, in the future, your dancing skills receive ample opportunity for use."

For a moment it seemed she was at a loss. Damn, but he'd offended her. She'd obviously not wanted to dance, yet he'd practically dragged her out here. She was still grieving—this waltz he'd insisted on was in very bad taste. He should never have insisted.

"Thank you, sir," she said finally, gazing at the floor. "But you are too kind. "

"I am not kind, Miss Maitland," he said, and wished it were not so very accurate. "I think you shall find I am not kind at all."

A kind man would never have swooped in and made her agree to marry him so soon after she lost Larry. A kind man would have found a way to aid and protect her from

Larry's behavior, not use it to his advantage. A kind man would never hold her so tightly and be just the slightest bit grateful that his cousin was gone and he could have her for his own.

No, he wasn't any sort of *kind*.

"Your words, at least, are kind," she said. "And I value that. Perhaps..."

He waited for her to go on, but she did not.

"Perhaps?"

"Er... perhaps when this dance is over, you might sit and talk with me for a moment?" she asked.

"But of course," he replied. "I should like that. Anything in particular you wish to discuss?"

"We are about to be married, sir," she said. "I should hope you could imagine there might be a few things we should discuss."

"I can think of a great number of things we ought to discuss," he replied. "And a few more that would, perhaps, be better if demonstrated."

Her cheeks colored vividly. "I think simple discussion will do for right now, my lord."

"If that is your wish," he said, forcing himself to get all notions of demonstration out of his head. "I always aim to do my duty."

"Yes, you do excel in that," she said with a noticeable sigh.

He hoped there would be many more times in their future when he could cause her to sigh. This sigh, however, did not have quite the timbre he would generally hope for. He heard far too much sorrow in it. Letting her drift into silence, he held her close as they danced. In time, much of her sadness for Larry would ebb away. He would be there for her when she was ready for him. The fact that she wanted to talk to him tonight seemed wonderfully promising.

*   *   *

The dance continued on, but she could think of nothing more to say to him. *Duty.* That was what this was to him and he was applying himself just as he ought. It would be so easy for her to forget he did not really want her!

But she had her own duty, and that was to be fully honest with him and set him free. And she would do that, just as soon as this heavenly dance was over. She'd get him alone and tell him they would not be married. She hoped he might be slightly disappointed, but most likely he would thank her politely then go on about his life. He'd probably be back on the dance floor, doing his *duty* with someone well-connected and beautiful like that dratted Miss Amelie D'Arnaud. She prayed God that by that time, she would be home weeping in her pillow and not forced to watch.

The music was drawing to the end of the waltz and she was horribly conflicted inside. She wanted to stay like this, held in his arms being whirled around the room, but at the same time she was eager to end the charade. As soon as it was proper, she pressed herself away from him and tried to smile.

"A fine dance, sir. Thank you. We should go talk now."

"Very well. Perhaps you'd like some refreshment?"

"Yes, thank you."

She allowed him to lead her toward the refreshment room. They could find a quiet place to sit there. She could break their engagement and sip lemonade casually. There'd be others around so perhaps, for the sake of appearance, he might not let his joy show too plainly on his face when she released him.

They were barely through the threshold of the smaller room where tables had been set up for refreshment and chairs lined the walls when Mrs. Plunket appeared at her side. A small pack of her matronly friends surrounded her.

"What a beautiful couple you make!" one of the ladies crooned.

Netta knew the woman as Mrs. Boosley. She also knew that it was highly unlikely they would be able to escape from her any time soon.

"Just watching the two of you takes me back to my own days as a young bride... ah, such happy times then."

Another one of the ladies chortled knowingly. "We never had the benefit of the waltz back in our day, you know. Our gentlemen had to wait until after the wedding to put their hands on us, dearie."

All the older women tittered. Lord Gladbourne shuffled nervously and Netta wished she had never been born. What awkwardness! With such an audience, she would never be able to get out of this engagement.

"Goodness, but the poor thing has been danced breathless," Mrs. Plunket exclaimed. "You should be more careful of her, my lord. Just look how flushed she is. Come, Miss Maitland. Sit over here with us while your gentleman fetches a lemonade."

Netta glanced up at Gladbourne, horrified that her companion should expect him to dance to her bidding. But he simply gave the older woman a gracious bow and smiled politely. As always, his sense of duty ruled the situation.

"But of course I will be her errand boy, ma'am. Please, make yourself comfortable, Miss Maitland. I will attend you instantly."

Every kindness he showed her just grated at her soul. It had been everything she ever wanted! What bitterness to be receiving it now, but for all the wrong reasons. She could take no more of it. To be surrounded by these coy matrons while he feigned doting concern... she feared she would burst into tears at any moment.

"Thank you, my lord, but I would hate to keep you from

your guests. You must go back to the dancing. I will sit with Mrs. Plunket for a while."

He blinked at her, his face showing just for a moment that she'd surprised him. But then his usual mask was firmly in place and he gave a polite bow.

"Very well, Miss Maitland. If you are sure you have no further need of me?"

"No. None. Thank you, sir."

"In that case, I will look in on you again."

"Thank you, but there is no need. Mrs. Plunket will see that I am well."

"I see," he replied. "In that case, I do hope you enjoy the remainder of your evening."

"Thank you, sir. And you, as well."

*   *   *

Gladbourne recognized a dismissal when he heard one. Hellfire, but it seemed Miss Maitland could suddenly not be rid of him quick enough. She maneuvered herself into the middle of the group of cackling biddies and was out of his reach in a second. The ladies thought her missishness was endearing and they happily took her under their wings. He merely wished he could see Netta's behavior as the jitters of a soon-to-be bride.

Suddenly her request for "a talk" made unfortunate sense. She had not been planning to get him alone to prepare for their wedding; she was planning to cut him loose. She had not felt what he felt as they danced. She was preparing to break their engagement. It was written over her face and evident in everything she had said. He'd been a simpleton not to see it.

Miss Maitland did not want him.

He could hardly fault her, of course. She was in love with Larry. How could he possibly have thought that might

30

change simply because Larry was dead?

More than anyone, he ought to understand that losing one's heart to someone had very little to do with how much they might love in return. He'd been in love with Netta for some time, though she'd never given any hint of reciprocation.

He needed to leave here. There was French brandy back in his rooms and tonight seemed as good a night as any to drain the decanter. He knew what Miss Maitland wanted and he would give it to her. Tomorrow, if she wished it, he'd walk away. He'd let society brand him the worse sort of cad and he'd bear all the blame, but she could be free. He could not give back her Larry, but he sure as hell did not need to saddle her with a lovesick husband who, at best, she might someday come to pity.

He was so lost in his own dark cloud that he very nearly walked right into a young woman. He excused himself and tried to move around her, but she practically clung to him. When he finally met her dark, almond shaped eyes, he was surprised to find recognition and something close to desperation in them.

"Forgive me, Lord Gladbourne," she said with just the hint of an accent he did not recognize. "But I must speak to you. Privately."

Her lowered voice and the intensity of emotion behind her eyes stopped him. He was quite certain he'd never seen this woman in his life, but she certainly knew him. What the devil sort of game was this?

"I'm sorry, miss. Have we been introduced?"

She pulled nervously at the fabric of her rumpled gown and glanced over her shoulder. "No sir, but please let me speak with you. It is of a matter most grave."

"Are you in some sort of trouble, miss?"

"No, it is a private matter. Regarding..." She dropped her voice even lower and leaned in, those dark exotic eyes flashing. "Your cousin, Laurence Granville."

Alarm bells rang out in his head. A desperate young woman seeking his help in a private matter regarding his bounder of a cousin? Hellfire, he could only imagine where this might be going. Had Larry left this woman in a delicate condition? Is that why the stupid fool had been so desperate to rid himself of Miss Maitland? Clearly Gladbourne had never known his cousin half as well as he thought that he had.

"I'm sorry, miss, but I may have some startling news for you. My cousin, unfortunately, is dead."

She shook her head vehemently. "That is what I need to tell you, sir. He is alive! And I need you to find him before he does something drastic."

He could not imagine what was more drastic than what Larry had already done, but before he could comment further the young woman thrust a letter into his hands. One glance quickly caught his attention. The handwriting scrawled across it was Larry's. Moreover, the date written at the top could not be ignored.

Laurence Garville had written this letter two days after he died.

Chapter 4

Netta tried not to watch him as he left her. She'd told him to go, so why should she feel as if he were abandoning her? She had cravenly not extricated herself from the ladies and she'd sent him off. Lord Gladbourne's tall, elegant form was walking away from her and she hadn't yet told him they were no longer engaged.

But wait, he was pausing. Maybe he was returning! Perhaps he realized she did not want to be alone with these pattering matrons, after all. She peered up through her lashes as she tried to keep her eyes modestly downcast and watched. He stood just inside the doorway.

He did not turn around and come back to them, though. No, he was with a young woman. Who was she? She was standing so close to Gladbourne that Netta could barely see her. Either the young lady was intentionally trying to keep herself hidden, or she and his lordship were very well acquainted. Netta simmered inside.

Another beautiful woman? Obviously he was not allowing his engagement to put any damper on his social calendar. She should have broken with him despite the tittering gawkers.

The dark-haired miss had his full attention now. What was this she handed him? *A letter.* Netta did not even wish to imagine what might be inside. She hardly had to wonder, though. The dark, smoky expression that came over Gladbourne's face as he read it told her more than enough. He was thoroughly intrigued. The girl whispered something to him and went off in a hurry. Unsurprising, Gladbourne followed without so much as a glance over his shoulder.

Drat! Not only was the man being blatantly unfaithful,

but he hadn't come back into the room and allowed Netta to break his heart. If he had one, which was doubtful. It seemed his primary organ lay somewhere other than behind his chest.

Well, if he wanted to dally with Miss D'Arnaud, or this brunette, or every other female at the ball tonight, he was going to have to be properly jilted first. Netta would find him and tell him exactly what she thought of his rakish ways and his wandering eye for everyone except her. She was not merely some duty that he was obliged to—she deserved a proper husband, or none at all. She would rather be scandalized by a suicidal fiancé than by a philandering one.

"Excuse me, Mrs. Plunket," she said, popping up to her feet and startling the other ladies. "I just recalled an urgent matter I forgot to mention to Lord Gladbourne."

The ladies must have had some silly notions what this urgent matter could be because they all started tittering even more gratingly than before. Netta tried not to let them see her cringe. It was not their fault she was out of sorts. It was her own fault for allowing stupid, syrupy sentiment for Lord Gladbourne to rule her thoughts.

Well, no more. He wasn't really hers and he never would be. It would be better for both of them if she sucked up her courage and ended this thing now—after she interrupted his brunette.

She rather carelessly took her leave of the ladies and hurried off in the direction she had seen Gladbourne going. It was a lucky thing she hurried, too. As she passed through the doorway from the refreshment room back into the ballroom she just barely caught a glimpse of him ducking behind a large fern. Good heavens, was he planning on tupping his lady right there, under the noses of the ball goers?

Ah, no he wasn't. As she maneuvered through the crowded room, clinging to the perimeter to avoid the dancers reveling in a lively country dance, she could begin to see that the potted fern was placed before the entrance to a corridor. Gladbourne and the woman had gone that way, out from under the noses of the ball goers.

She followed. At least, she tried to follow. Everyone she passed seemed to want to stop her and give her well wishes. She was as gracious as she could be yet still kept making her way. By the time she finally reached the fern to peer through its fronds, the corridor appeared empty. And dark.

She slipped behind the fern anyway. Where did the couple go? She listened over the ballroom din to detect the sound of Lord Gladbourne's boots. She couldn't detect them, though.

This corridor appeared to be an access for servants. At the far end was a dark opening that must lead to a staircase, probably going down to the kitchens. On her left were two doors, both shut. On her right was one door that opened to the outside. It was slightly ajar. Obviously her quarry had gone that way, so she followed.

She wished she had grabbed up her wrap as the chilly night air prickled her skin. Would the dark-haired girl complain about that? Would Gladbourne graciously warm her? Perhaps it was best not to think of such things.

The door had opened onto a narrow walkway. She could see no sign of anyone, so she followed the walkway around to the rear of the building. There was not much there, just a dark, dirty alleyway adjoining the mews. Her nose wrinkled on impulse. In the distance horses neighed and a dog barked.

There was no sign of Lord Gladbourne, though. She was about to turn back when movement in the shadows caught her attention. Her eyes narrowed and tried to see into the blackness. Yes... someone was there...

"Who is it?" she called.

"Netta?"

"Yes, but who..."

The voice had been familiar, but of course she must be mistaken. For a moment she could have sworn it sounded exactly like...

"Larry!"

Oh, by God it was him. He stepped into the pool of moonlight beside her and she staggered back. She stared at him until she was certain her eyes were not playing tricks. Then she threw her arms around him.

"You aren't gone! You're still in London!"

He embraced her in response. "Yes, things didn't go quite as I had planned."

"But of course they did. Everyone thinks you are dead!"

"It was a cruel, selfish thing for me to do, Netta," he said, putting her from him and meeting her with such a serious expression she began to worry a bit.

"You had other plans," she reminded him. "We didn't wish to marry each other."

He shook his head. "As I recall, you didn't wish to marry *anyone* and now... well, you're even worse off than before. You're being forced to marry my cousin!"

"He and my father thought the scandal from what happened might hurt my reputation. I tried to convince them I didn't mind if I was removed from polite society, but—"

"Of course they couldn't let that happen to you. I'm sorry, I should have realized how this would affect you. Gladbourne did the right thing, and I... well, I did not."

"It doesn't matter," she assured him, reaching to hug him again.

"It *does* matter," another voice said.

36

This was not Larry. Someone else had joined them. *Gladbourne*!

"Er, hello, cousin," Larry said.

Gladbourne practically flew at him, not for a joyous embrace, but to grab poor Larry by the throat and begin shaking him.

"What the hell are you doing here? You're supposed to be dead!"

Larry may have tried to say something, but the garbled sounds that he uttered were not precisely words. It didn't matter. Gladbourne ranted on for him.

"You have the nerve to show up and present yourself to Miss Maitland? Do you have any idea what you've put her through this past month?"

The way the earl was shaking his cousin, it seemed he was intent on putting her through it again, in reality this time. She was forced to lay her hands on him and beg him to stop.

"Please, sir! Don't kill him. He... he isn't the only one at fault here."

Gladbourne somehow heard her pleas and released his hold on Larry. He turned to peer at her with dark, fiery eyes. Larry gasped for air.

"I am sorry, Miss Maitland," Gladbourne said, a ferocious edge evident in his voice. "I forget that you still care for this scoundrel, even after he put on such a horrible display and deceived you so abominably."

"But he didn't deceive me," she said, wishing she didn't have to continue, but helpless to lie to Gladbourne any longer. "I knew he wasn't truly dead."

Gladbourne blinked, incredulous. "You knew?"

"Yes, and I'm so very sorry for everything that I did."

"Everything that *you* did?"

"No, this wasn't her fault," Larry said quickly. "It was all *my* doing. I had some foolish notion of... well, that hardly matters now. Miss Maitland and I were being pushed into marriage and we both wanted a way out, so I invented this scheme."

Instead of railing at Larry, or pressing him for a better explanation, Gladbourne turned a questioning gaze onto Netta. "You did not wish to marry him?"

"No, sir," she replied. "Our families arranged it, but I did not wish to be married, not to Larry... not to anyone."

"And yet you agreed to be married to me," Gladbourne pointed out.

She couldn't quite meet his eyes. Surely he would see her hypocrisy, her willingness to let him throw himself away on a marriage he didn't want all the while he grieved a cousin she knew was not dead. He would have every reason to hate her after this.

"I'm sorry," was all she could murmur.

"This is why I had to rise from the dead," Larry announced. "I couldn't let her be forced into a marriage she detested."

"Detested?" Gladbourne sounded honestly hurt. "You detest me, Miss Maitland? Truly, I had no idea your feelings on this matter were so strong. I was simply stepping up to save you from the censure we feared you would face due to *his* reprehensible actions."

"There's no need to harp on that, cousin" Larry said. "I am here repenting of my sins. I should have just married Miss Maitland as I was supposed to, so here I am and that's what I'll do."

"You're going to marry her after all?" Gladbourne asked.

"Yes. I'm the one who brought scandal on her, so I ought to be the one to suffer for it."

"*Suffer* for it?" Netta snapped.

Well! Larry could have certainly chosen a less

offensive phrase. How dare he think she'd even consider him at this point? She would have told him so, too, except that he was too busy arguing with his cousin to notice her frustration.

"You can't marry her," Gladbourne declared. "She's currently engaged to *me*."

"But she doesn't want to marry you," Larry noted.

"She admitted she doesn't want to marry you either," Gladbourne pointed out, then added, "Moreover, you don't even love her."

Larry was quick to counter. "Well, neither do you."

Gladbourne just glared at him. "What do you know of my feelings for her? You've been presumed dead."

"Yes, and what has been your excuse for ignoring her all this time?" Larry asked. "I thought she was safely out of the parson's clutches and on her way to the quiet life in the country she's always wanted. I could scarce believe it when I learned you are set to marry her! You've barely had anything to do with her since... well, since you and her father arranged our betrothal."

"Of course I've barely had anything to do with her," Gladbourne said with a scowl. "She was your fiancée. I could hardly be playing suitor then, could I?"

"Well, there's no need for you to keep playing now," Larry said, moving to Netta's side. "I've come back and I'll do my duty. I'll marry Netta."

"Like hell you will!" Gladbourne said, grabbing his cousin again and pulling him away. "If she was so eager to be rid of you that she helped stage your suicide, then I doubt she'll welcome your purported return to sanity now."

"Are you questioning my mental stability?"

"Questioning it? No, cousin, I'm very sincerely doubting it. Miss Maitland deserves something better. She deserves..."

"She deserves what?" Larry asked. "She deserves *you*?"

39

Netta held her breath, not at all sure what Gladbourne might reply but knowing very much what she'd like to hear. In the end, the man simply exhaled and shook his head.

"No, she deserves better than either of us. She deserves better than being pressured into marriage out of some sense of obligation or duty, and she most certainly deserves better than you running off to hide at Aunt Tabitha's house while the rest of us assumed you dead."

Netta wasn't at all certain who this Aunt Tabitha was, but Larry seemed quite struck by it.

"How do you know about that?" he asked sharply.

Gladbourne barely seemed to care. "Some little dark-haired chit approached me indoors and showed me your letter."

Larry's eyes grew huge and now it was his turn to grab his cousin by the coat and shake him for answers.

"She was *here*? When? Where is she now?"

Gladbourned shoved him away. "A few minutes ago. She insisted on speaking in private with me, then seemed in a hurry, so she ran off."

"I've got to find her!" Larry was suddenly a bundle of nervous energy. He turned to Netta and grabbed up her hands, squeezing them tightly. "I'm sorry, so sorry, Netta. I can't marry you now."

"Er... I thought that was already decided?" she replied, very confused.

He dropped her hands and stepped away, giving Gladbourne a long, searing look. "Be good to her, cousin. Or you'll answer to me."

"But what are—"

"I have to go," Larry said quickly.

He gave one final, sheepish glance at Netta, then dashed off into the shadows. They were left in silence as the sound of his hurrying footsteps faded in the distance.

Finally Netta dared to glance up at Gladbourne.

"What do you suppose that was all about?" she asked.

He shook his head. "I haven't a clue, but I daresay we'll get that story later. For right now, I'm much more concerned with *your* story, Miss Maitland."

"My story?"

"How should it end? Did you really wish to be rid of Larry so that you could retire alone to the countryside?"

"Er, yes... that is what I intended when I agreed to help him disappear..."

"And yet you ended up engaged to me."

She felt her cheeks growing warm. "I'm very sorry, sir. I know it was not what you wished, but I just somehow never got around to turning you down."

"Why should you think it was not what I wished?"

"Well, you made is so very clear that you were simply doing your duty, that you felt marrying me was nothing more than an obligation that you would much rather have avoided."

"And yet you were willing to let me go through with it."

"I know... I am so very sorry. I was cruel to trap you into a marriage you did not want."

He had moved very close to her and his eyes held a fire she could not look away from. "That is not at all what I was trapped in, Miss Maitland. It is I who should apologize to you. Just say the word now and I will release you forever."

His voice was barely a murmur in the night breeze. He was so near to her she could feel the heat from his body. It prickled her skin and made her feel warm all over. She gazed up at him, helpless to find words yet desperate to beg him never to leave her.

"Speak the words, Netta," he repeated. "Tell me to leave and I will never bother you again."

Her throat was so tight and so dry that she could not have said anything if her life depended on it. Indeed, just now she felt that it did. How could she go on living if there was a chance he might care for her and she could not express her own sentiments? The silence was agonizing.

"Er... you'd best speak those words quickly," he advised her. "I'm just about to pull you into my arms and kiss you. It won't be a mild, chaste little kiss, either."

Her heart nearly pounded out of her chest. At last she found breath to say something.

"I think I would like that, sir."

Now he exhaled as if he'd been storing up all the air in the city. "Ah, thank God, then."

Without hesitation, he made good on his threat. He wrapped her into his arms and held her tightly while his lips found hers and he kissed her boldly. Indeed, there was nothing at all chaste about his kiss. She liked it immensely. Thank heavens they were getting married tomorrow! After kisses like this, she would be every bit as ruined and scandalized as Papa had worried her previous engagement had left her.

She would always owe a debt to dear Larry and his reckless plot. Somehow through it all, she'd ended up with her heart's desire. True love might survive an unloaded pistol and a hastily staged explosion, but one well-aimed shot from Cupid's bow was decidedly terminal.

Susan Gee Heino

The Elegant Scheme to Marry Lord Larry

A Regency Short Story

by Susan Gee Heino

Dedication

To Jack.
I'm really glad all our scheming worked.

Chapter 1

London, England, May, 1817

Cristina Maria Magdalena Alvarez del Reyes was perfectly at home in these elegant Mayfair rooms. True, her family heritage and exotic name would forever mark her as not quite a proper English miss, but on first glance she blended in perfectly with the fashionable set around her. She was not the only English lady with raven hair and dark eyes, and no one could ever fault her speech—English was her natural tongue, after all.

Why should it not be? She had been raised here on her mother's native soil for most of her life. Indeed, her father had insisted on frequent trips to his homeland when the political environment would allow, but she'd been born, raised, and educated in the bosom of her mother's people. Gentle people. Fashionable, respectable, and oh, so very English.

She'd expected to spend the rest of her life here with them, in fact. She'd planned to marry, raise a family, and grow old right here in England. It was most unfortunate, then, that the gentleman she'd planned to marry and grow old with had gone off and killed himself.

"I can't believe you are actually here!" her friend, Amelie D'Arnaud, exclaimed in hushed tones, glancing over her shoulder and positioning herself as if to shield Cristina from discovery by the crush populating the ballroom. "I thought your family had gone back to Spain?"

"Indeed we did. It's just that... I decided not to stay

47

there. So I returned."

"You returned? Not your family?"

"My family was not precisely consulted on the matter."

"You can't mean... you came back to England *alone*?"

Cristina cringed. Her friend made it sound so very scandalous.

Which it was, of course.

"Shush! Please, Amelie, I don't have much time. I need to find Lord Gladbourne."

"Gladbourne? But he's... oh, Cristina! He's your fiancé's cousin. Is that why you've come back? You still cannot reconcile yourself to what Lord Larry has done?"

"I most certainly have not reconciled myself to it," Cristina replied, and wished she had the time to explain things.

But she did not. Her father had followed her back to England and even now he was hunting her in the city. No doubt he and that foppish Spaniard that Papá wished for her to marry were close on her heels. It was only a matter of time before she was apprehended and dragged back to their home. Papá would likely chain her in her room after this show of reckless behavior.

Drat her fiancé. She loved him dearly, but what could her precious Lord Larry have been thinking? Didn't he realize how she would suffer when news came of what he had done? Had he no notion of the anguish his actions would put her through?

Apparently he did not. Stupid man. She was in quite a mind of boxing his ears when she saw him again.

And she *would* see him again. Soon. It was the very reason she was here in London now, six weeks after his traumatic death.

Amelie clearly did not understand. "But this is Lord Gladbourne's engagement party, Cristina. You can't mean to ruin this happy occasion by reminding him of his dead cousin, can you?"

"I'm hoping to make the day a good deal happier for him, actually."

"So you do not intend to involve his cousin?"

"Involve him?" Cristina almost laughed at her friend's unwitting prophecy. "I fully intend to prop him in a chair, gaze into his soul-less eyes, and berate him with very harsh language. I might even raise my voice at him. Lord knows the scoundrel deserves it."

Now Amelie appeared horrified. "You are quite mad!"

"Calm yourself," Cristina advised, glancing beyond Amelie to find Lord Gladbourne in the crowd. "It is all far less macabre than it might sound. I will explain everything later. Right now, I must go speak to our host."

Poor Amelie was in too much shock to do much of anything as Cristina pushed past her and set a direct course for the tall figure of Gladbourne. He was, indeed, enjoying this festive occasion and his eyes were fixed securely on his fetching young bride as he left her in the company of several older ladies. Cristina had to sidle up next to him and lay her hand on his arm to even get his attention. He turned a questioning gaze on her and she very nearly lost her nerve.

The man's resemblance to Larry was striking. Gladbourne was a bit older, but his features were familiar. He lacked the playfulness she had come to know in Larry, though, and the set of his jaw made her feel suddenly small and inferior. What if he didn't believe her? Or worse, what if he *did* believe her and accused her of perpetrating a cruel and painful scheme?

It suddenly dawned on her that this meeting might not be such a very good idea, after all. But it was too late to run away now. The gentleman was trying to push his way past her.

"Excuse me, miss," he said.

She didn't budge, though, determined to remain very much in his way.

"Forgive me, Lord Gladbourne, but I must speak to you. Privately."

His brow furrowed and his eyes were dark. "I'm sorry, miss. Have we been introduced?"

She pulled nervously at the fabric of her rumpled gown and glanced over her shoulder. "No sir, but please let me speak with you. It is of a matter most grave."

"Are you in some sort of trouble, miss?"

"No, it is a private matter. Regarding..." She dropped her voice even lower and leaned in closer. "Your cousin, Laurence Granville."

"I'm sorry, miss," he said. His voice was cold and his eyes even colder. "But I may have some startling news for you. My cousin, unfortunately, is dead."

"That is what I need to tell you, sir," she replied quickly, gathering her nerve so she could continue. "He is alive! And I need you to find him before he does something drastic."

With that, she thrust a letter into his hands. The man unfolded it and after one glance she knew he recognized the handwriting. She watched his eyes shift as he studied the page. His attention quickly settled on the date scrawled in a corner. She knew he could hardly ignore that.

Laurence Garville had written this letter two days *after* he'd supposedly committed suicide.

"This was written to you?" he asked after a moment.

"Yes. I am Cristina Maria Magdalena Alvarez del Reyes. Can we discuss this in private, please?"

The last thing she needed was to be seen or overheard. Across the room she had noticed a corridor, partially hidden by potted foliage used for decoration. They could continue the discussion there.

Lord Gladbourne was obviously intrigued and he nodded, letting her lead the way. She was quite out of breath from nerves when they ducked around dancers and slid into the shadows of the corridor. A doorway opened into a closet. It seemed the perfect place for such a sensitive conversation.

"What is this, Miss del Reyes?" Gladbourned asked when they were alone. "What scheme are you playing at?"

"It's no scheme, sir," she replied. "I want the truth just as much as I'm sure you do."

"I thought I already had that."

"As did I, sir, until I received this letter."

He still held it, glancing over it again despite the dim light in their little room.

"It is my cousin's hand," he acknowledged. "What is your involvement with him?"

"Your cousin and I were secretly engaged to be married."

The man was no dullard. Understanding washed over his expression and one dark eyebrow arched sharply.

"You realize he was not-so-secretly also engaged to Miss Maitland?"

"I realize it now, sir. Prior to sending this letter, however, Larry had failed to mention that little fact."

His lordship swore under his breath. He didn't seem nearly as happy as she'd hoped he would be to learn that this past month of mourning for Larry's tragic demise had, in fact, been a bit premature. This letter carried proof that Larry, it turned out, was not quite as dead as they'd all initially believed.

"So you knew nothing of my cousin's plans?"

"No sir," she assured him. "I heard of Larry's death at my home in Essex. It was quite a shock, and my father was furious that I'd committed myself to a man he hadn't approved. Within the next days Papá took our whole family to Spain. This letter followed us there and only recently made its way to me."

"So this is true?" he questioned, looking over the letter again.

"That is what I wanted to ask you," she replied. "You were there when he... when he did what he did. Do you believe this could be true?"

She'd heard the story of Larry's dramatic death from her own cousin, Roland Bentley. He was close friend of Larry's and, in fact, had been the one who introduced them. When the horrible events transpired in London just over a month ago, Roland had hurried to Essex to inform Cristina. She'd had no reason to doubt him and was certain he'd been reporting things as he believed them to be.

After Roland's report, she'd found verification in Papá's newspapers. Everyone was talking of it. Larry Garville, heir to the Earl of Idling, had committed suicide. It was a sordid tale and everyone was captivated by it.

Lord Larry, as they called him, had gotten himself engaged to two women at the same time. Trapped and remorseful, he'd resorted to desperate actions. It hadn't ended well. He'd abducted his other fiancée, Miss Maitland, and threatened to kill her. Then he turned the violence on himself, letting Miss Maitland go and wildly vowing suicide.

By all accounts, Lord Gladbourne had tried to save him, but Larry retreated to a boat in the Thames where he was witnessed taking his own life. The boat exploded and burned, sinking into the river and taking Larry's body with it. He was never seen again.

The stories left out none of the awful details and probably embellished a few. Cristina had wept tears of agony, picturing the events over and over again and wondering what she could have done to stop him. If he ever had loved her, how could he possibly do this?

That question was even more poignant now that she had received this letter.

"The letter indicates that everything I thought I had witnessed was a carefully planned ruse," Lord Gladbourne said.

"Was it?" she asked, terrified of his answer.

From the moment she received Larry's letter she had wanted to believe it, had prayed it was true. Larry explained everything, how he intended to fake an abduction and convince the world he'd gone mad. He'd staged it all, including the fire that would make recovery of a body impossible. Then he was planning to carry Cristina away so they could live happily ever after.

Unfortunately, with Shakespearean pathos, she had not gotten word of his plan until it was too late.

She'd thought him dead, so she'd let Papa take her to Spain and promise her to the man of his choosing. What did it matter whom she married now that Larry was gone? She'd agreed to make her father happy.

Larry, however, had been expecting a reply. He hadn't known she wouldn't be in Essex to receive his letter. He'd ask her to meet him if she wanted the life he offered. Otherwise, he claimed he would sail to America and never bother her again. By the time she finally got his letter, it was entirely possible he thought he'd been rejected and had gone off without her.

Whether he was alive or dead, she truly might never see him again.

"It is possible," Lord Gladbourne said at last. "I was some distance from my cousin when he... when things occurred. I was fully convinced at the time, but if it really was just some ghastly ruse designed to deceive, it is possible I was duped."

Cristina's heart fluttered inside her. Gladbourned confirmed what she longed to hear. Larry was still alive! She could still get the chance to box his fool ears, after all. If only he had not gone away.

"Please, sir, where do you think he might be?" she begged Gladbourne. "I need to find him right away."

Gladbourne scowled. "I don't know, but I promise you he *will* be found. When I get my hands on the devious bounder, he'll wish he'd gone through with things in earnest."

Chapter 2

Larry wished he were dead. He'd been the biggest fool in the world, thinking his idiotic scheme full of lies and deception could somehow result in any sort of happiness. Of course Cristina had not wanted to run away with him. What could have possessed him to even ask such a thing of her?

He'd been nothing less than a coward to concoct his ridiculous plot, and he'd been a pure blackguard to carry it out. It was no wonder he'd heard nothing from Cristina after he sent her that letter. She deserved much better than the scandal and shame that he offered.

But he'd been desperate. His family had always expected him to marry Netta Maitland and, until he met Cristina, it had never dawned on him to consider anyone else. He and Netta had grown up together; she was his dearest friend. The last thing he wanted to do was hurt her, but she was far more a sister to him than she could ever be a wife.

When he'd finally confided in her, he'd been relieved to discover she was no more inclined toward him than he was toward her. Unfortunately, Cristina's father was equally un-inclined toward Larry. He wanted Cristina to marry one of the Grandees from his homeland, not some spineless Englishman who had the bad form to break a long-standing engagement with the perfectly respectable Miss Maitland.

Larry should have known that instead of running away with him in shame, Cristina would do what was proper and right. Larry had waited more than a fortnight after he sent that letter asking her to meet him at his Aunt Tabitha's house so they could spirit away. When no reply came to him, he swallowed his pride and went to her home in Essex to give her opportunity to refuse him in person. He was told then that the family had gone to Spain and that Cristina was now engaged to a man there.

His stupid plan had made her hate him and she'd left the country rather than have to face him. He spent the next two weeks too drunk to care, but eventually even that was not enough to ease his pain. He was ashamed of himself and knew there was only one thing he could do if he ever wanted to face himself in the mirror again.

He sobered up, came back to London, and was determined to redeem himself. He would start by confessing his folly to his cousin, and making sure that his former fiancée was happily living the quite life of spinsterhood that she'd desperately wanted.

It came as quite a surprise, then, when he learned that his cousin was about to be married to Netta. Poor Netta! She didn't want to marry anyone, let alone his overbearing, boorish cousin Gladbourne.

Fortunately Larry had arrived just in time. He couldn't secure his own future happiness, but he certainly would secure Netta's. He owed her that much, at least.

First he had to find a respectable way to let everyone know he wasn't dead. Showing up at his cousin's ball tonight might be a bit overly dramatic, but with the wedding scheduled for tomorrow morning, Larry had no other option. With luck, he could find Gladbourne alone and speak to him privately.

Creeping up the narrow alleyway behind the fine house that hosted the ball, Larry ducked into a shadow when he noticed a figure leaving a rear entrance. Lamplight and the sounds of laughter and music spilled out the open windows, but the walkway behind the building was dark and secluded. Larry peered around the corner to get a closer look at the lone figure.

He recognized her immediately and was more than a little surprised. An involuntary curse escaped him.

"Who is it?" she called out into the darkness.

"Netta?" He spoke her name, not quite sure how she would greet him after he'd involved her in his pretended suicide and the subsequent scandal.

"Yes, but who..." His former fiancée paused only a moment and then it was obvious she recognized his voice. "Larry!"

She actually sounded happy to find him here, so he stepped out into a splash of moonlight. She blinked in disbelief at him for a moment, then smiled and threw her arms around his neck.

"You aren't gone! You're still in London!"

He embraced her in response. "Yes, things didn't go quite as I had planned."

"But of course they did. Everyone thinks you are dead!"

"It was a cruel, selfish thing for me to do, Netta," he said, and wished for all the world he could instantly undo it.

"You had other plans," she reminded him. "We didn't wish to marry each other."

"As I recall, you didn't wish to marry *anyone* and now... well, you're even worse off than before. You're being forced to marry my cousin!"

She obviously couldn't meet his eyes and pulled away from him now. He could have kicked himself for not realizing what his scheme would likely do to her.

"He and my father thought the scandal from what happened might hurt my reputation," she explained. "I tried to convince them I didn't mind if I was removed from polite society, but—"

"Of course they couldn't let that happen to you," he interrupted quickly, hating himself more than ever. "I'm sorry, I should have realized how this would affect you. Gladbourne did the right thing, and I... well, I did not."

"It doesn't matter," she assured him, reaching to hug him again.

"It *does* matter," another voice said.

Damn it. Another figure had come out of the building and Larry recognized this one, too. *Gladbourne.*

"Er, hello, cousin," Larry greeted with very false cheerfulness.

There was nothing false about his cousin's reaction. The anger and hatred were entirely sincere as Gladbourne flew at him, grabbing Larry's collar and shaking him.

"What the hell are you doing here? You're supposed to be dead!"

Larry did his best to keep breathing while Gladbourne made an obvious attempt to choke the life out of him. He ranted on about Larry's deceit and how his idiocy had heaped shame and suffering all over Netta. Larry supposed he could have fought the man off, but he honestly deserved a good thrashing so he put up with it.

Netta, however, was always kind hearted. She begged Gladbourne to release him. Oddly enough, her words had an effect and next thing Larry knew, he could get air again and the world was no longer spinning around him.

"I am sorry, Miss Maitland," Gladbourne grumbled. "I forget that you still care for this scoundrel, even after he put on such a horrible display and deceived you so abominably."

Larry was still trying to find his voice when Netta plowed into a confession. Before he could stop her, she told Gladbourne the truth. She admitted that she'd known all along Larry wasn't dead and that she'd been a part of his deception.

Gladbourne blinked at her, incredulous. "You knew?"

"No, this wasn't her fault," Larry declared, eager to defend her.

It was true, none of this was Netta's fault. He'd dragged her into it. If Gladbourne should be angry at anyone, it should not be Netta. Larry would have to do some thrashing of his own if Gladbourne showed any antagonism toward Netta. When the man turned to her, though, his voice was quiet and questioning.

"You did not wish to marry him?"

"No, sir," she replied, shaking her head with some conviction. "Our families arranged it, but I did not wish to be married, not to Larry... not to anyone."

"And yet you agreed to be married to me," Gladbourne pointed out.

"I'm sorry," was all she could murmur.

The guilt and pain in her voice was wrenching. Larry was more furious with himself than ever. He'd been rash and selfish, and now look what had come of it. Cristina was marrying someone in Spain, he himself was broken-hearted and alone, and poor Netta was doomed to marry Gladbourne.

"*This* is why I had to rise from the dead," Larry announced. "I couldn't let her be forced into a marriage she detested."

Now Gladbourne's fury with him turned into something else. What was it? He seemed hurt, defeated. Larry was certain he'd never seen his cousin like this before.

"Detested?" Gladbourne said, turning back to Netta. "You *detest* me, Miss Maitland?"

Netta seemed not to know what to say, so Larry blathered on. He couldn't let her bear the brunt of this. If her reputation had been ruined by his actions, then he was the one who should marry her. It would never be a happy union, not like the one he'd envisioned with Cristina, but he could at least allow her to live the quiet life she wanted.

59

Before reason could talk him out of it, he declared his intentions and vowed to do the right thing by Netta.

"You're going to marry her after all?" Gladbourne asked him.

"Yes. I'm the one who brought scandal on her, so I ought to be the one to suffer for it."

Oddly enough, Netta was not as flattered by this as one might expect.

"*Suffer* for it?" she questioned.

Even more oddly, Gladbourne did not seem the least bit relieved to be let out of his matrimonial sentence.

"You can't marry her. She's currently engaged to *me*."

"But she doesn't want to marry you," Larry reminded him.

"She admitted she doesn't want to marry you either. Moreover, you don't even love her."

Love? When did this concept become part of the discussion? Of course Larry didn't love her. Gladbourne was diminishing his own argument by mentioning it.

"Well, neither do you."

"What do you know of my feelings for her?" Gladbourne growled. "You've been presumed dead."

They snipped and sniped at each other like children. What sort of ridiculousness was this? For every argument Larry offered that could provide Gladbourne an easy way out of his obligation to Netta, Gladbourned countered with passion. It was petty and unnecessary and the banter went long enough that Larry began to have an epiphany.

Gladbourned claimed he would marry Netta out of a sense of duty, but clearly there was more to it. Gladbourne wasn't lashing out because Larry had forced him into an unwanted marriage, he was angry that Larry had turned up to prevent it! When Galdbourne claimed that Netta deserved better than this, Larry knew exactly what

Gladbourne meant.

He threw it in his cousin's face. "She deserves *you*?"

Gladbourne was silent. Indeed, Larry had hit on the core of it. Amazing as it was, there could be no denying. Gladbourne had fallen in love with Netta.

Had Larry ever noticed any *tendre* forming there? He couldn't recall. Mostly, he'd been too preoccupied with daydreams of Cristina to pay any attention to any budding interest his cousin might have developed for Netta. Clearly, it was there, though.

Gladbourne's broad shoulders sagged. Despite the fact that Larry's throat still ached from the recent attempted choking, he suddenly felt incredibly sorry for his cousin. No one knew better than he how miserable it was to love a woman who did not return the emotion.

Gladbourne exhaled and shook his head slowly.

"No, she deserves better than either of us," he said. "She deserves better than being pressured into marriage out of some sense of obligation or duty, and she most certainly deserves better than you running off to hide at Aunt Tabitha's house while the rest of us assumed you dead."

Larry was caught entirely off guard by that last bit. Gladbourne knew he'd gone to Aunt Tabitha's house? But the house had been vacant; Aunt Tabitha had moved to her sister's and her staff was let go. Aside from that letter to Christina, Larry told know one where he was. There was no way Gladbourne could have this information.

"How do you know about that?" Larry demanded.

Gladbourne shrugged. "Some little dark-haired chit approached me indoors and showed me your letter."

Now it was Larry's turn to grab his cousin by the collar and shake him for answers.

"She was *here*? When? Where is she now?"

Gladbourned shoved him away and waved his hands in the direction of the building behind them. "A few minutes ago. She insisted on speaking in private with me, then seemed in a hurry, so she ran off."

Cristina. It could only be Cristina. Was it possible? Had she been here and he'd just missed her? Larry could barely contain his emotion.

"I've got to find her!" Larry said, grabbing Netta's hands and squeezing them tightly. "I'm sorry, so sorry, Netta. I can't marry you now."

"Er... I thought that was already decided?" she replied, wrinkling her brows.

Gladbourne moved closer to her and Larry glared at him. "Be good to her, cousin. Or you'll answer to me."

"But what are—"

There was no time for explanation. If Cristina had been here, she must not hate him as much as he thought she did. He had to go to her! But he couldn't. It would cause an uproar if a dead man went rushing into the ballroom. Besides, Gladbourne said she'd run off. Where would she go? Her mother's family... yes, her mother's family had a house right here in Mayfair. She must be there.

"I have to go," Larry said quickly.

He gave one last glance at Netta and was mildly amused to see that instead of moving away from Gladbourne as he hovered protectively over her, she nestled herself closer to him. Apparently Gladbourne wasn't the only one who'd developed tender emotions. Maybe Larry didn't need to worry for his dear little friend quite as much as he had been.

It was a liberating thought, but there was no time to dwell on it. He turned his back on them both and dashed off into the shadows. His footsteps echoed as he ran over the dirty stones, past the mews at the end of the narrow way, and out onto one of the darkened streets of the city. If Cristina was anywhere nearby, he'd find her.

Chapter 3

Cristina should not have been eavesdropping. Yes, because it was rude, but more importantly because of what she'd heard. She really, really wished she had not.

Larry was going to marry Miss Maitland! He'd come back from the dead specifically to steal her away from his cousin. Here Cristina was, running away from her family and endangering her life creeping about London at night and infiltrating balls that she was not invited to, all the while Larry was perfectly happy to forget her and marry the other girl.

Oh, but this was dreadful. The man's betrayal stung all the way to her core. Cristina had been hiding in that little room, waiting after Lord Gladbourne left her so that no one would see them leave such a secluded place together. She came out of the building through a back door and immediately realized she wasn't alone in this dark walkway. She hid in the shadows only to realize what she was witnessing.

Larry was there! And so was Miss Maitland. They'd been together, so it would seem, and Lord Gladbourne had found them. Now the two men were practically coming to blows, arguing over who would marry the girl. Larry appeared most passionate about it, too.

What nerve! The ink on his letter to Cristina, begging for her to abandon her life and run off with him, was barely dry. Now he was battling for Miss Maitland's hand?

It was the most horrible thing imaginable and Cristina felt her heart break in an instant. She didn't bother to stay to see who won the fight. What did it matter now that she knew the true fickleness of Larry? He could have his Miss

Maitland, for all Cristina cared. She ran back inside the building, not giving a fig for who might see as she darted through the crowd and out the front door.

Carriages lined the street and various footmen and drivers loitered about, laughing and enjoying their free time as they waited to carry the exhausted ball-goers home. Cristina couldn't see much of it, though. Tears blinded her and she struggled to maintain her composure.

One of the coachmen called to her, asking if she needed help locating her carriage. She dismissed him as quickly as she could, but now the others took note of her. A gangly footman in bright livery trotted up beside her as she hurried along. She knew how unseemly it was for a young woman to be seen alone this way. There was no telling how much further attention it might garner.

"Are you looking for someone, miss?" the footman asked.

"No, thank you. I am fine."

But obviously she wasn't fine and the footman did not leave off trailing her. She hoped it was purely out of concern for her well-being and not some other more nefarious goal. Her feet moved faster.

"Where are you bound for, miss?" he questioned. "I can call for someone to get you there."

"No need," she said, quickening her pace. "I prefer to walk."

And so she did. The footman finally gave up trying to keep pace with her. She didn't look back as she turned the corner at the end of the street and was glad to hear his footsteps cease behind her.

What on earth was she going to do with herself now that the man she had run away from her parents for didn't love her as much as she thought he did? Papá was surely close on her heels. What would he do when he found her cowering at Grandfather's townhouse? He'd rant and rave and probably force her to marry Don Bernardo the very moment a license could be procured. Then she'd be whisked back to Spain and be stuck there the rest of her life.

How dismal! She supposed the idea of that future shouldn't bother her as much as it did, considering that without Larry any future was dreary. She didn't hate Don Bernardo, and he certainly had been most proper in his treatment of her. Why should she not admit defeat and just go back to their home to await Papá? Don Bernardo was a wealthy, powerful man back in Spain. She would surely not suffer if she were his wife.

But she didn't want to be Don Bernardo's wife. She wanted to marry Larry.

He'd claimed to love her and she had believed him. She thought their connection had been real, something deeper than just passing fancy. Had she truly been so very wrong?

What nerve he had to lie to her, to make her love him, to put her through the misery of mourning him, to tease her with happiness, and then to decide on Miss Maitland after all. The mere injustice of it filled her with fury and she was, once more, plotting the sharp words she would have for him. Indeed, if she ever did get the opportunity to face him again she would... well, she would...

She would probably throw herself into his arms and weep like a toddler.

Drat, but she still loved the scoundrel, didn't she? She could never marry Don Bernardo or any other man. Her silly heart belonged to Larry and there was no altering that. She wanted him for herself and she always would.

And if she couldn't have him, why should Miss Maitland? That lady didn't need him. She was engaged to marry Lord Gladbourne. The wedding was set for tomorrow, for heaven's sake! Larry might try to sway her, but surely Miss Maitland did not care for Larry the way Cristina did. Obviously Miss Maitland hadn't wasted time finding another man once it seemed Larry was gone. She'd get over him again, unlike Cristina who was stupid enough to have lost her heart completely.

If Cristina was doomed to a lonely future of pining and spinsterhood, why should Larry end up happily wed to someone of his choosing? He shouldn't. Even if he didn't want Cristina after this, she could certainly see to it that he didn't get Miss Maitland.

Indeed, what would Miss Maitland think of her suitor if she knew that all the lovely things he likely whispered to her had already been whispered to someone else? Surely no woman would like that very much at all. In fact, the solidarity of womanhood demanded Cristina take action. Surely it behooved her to inform Miss Maitland just how many lovely things Larry had been whispering on his many secret visits to Essex.

Cristina glanced around and took stock of her location. She was not so far away from the house where the two lovers were meeting. She could turn up this very alleyway and follow it behind the buildings toward the mews, putting her in close proximity to the little garden area where Larry had been professing his love and begging Miss Maitland to give up his cousin. Perhaps the cousin, by now, had been vanquished and Larry was back at sweet talking.

Cristina's angry footsteps stopped in their tracks. She clenched her fists and ground her teeth. Yes, by heavens, she owed it to herself and to Miss Maitland not to merely walk away from this. Larry deserved whatever he had coming to him.

Stomping her foot, she turned off the street and scurried into the shadows. Rubbish and rats would not deter her. She would go back to that house and interrupt whatever Larry and his Miss Maitland were up to, and she would demand they listen as she recited Larry's many transgressions.

She would do that as long as she could before she melted into a teary heap and proved herself to be the biggest ninny in England.

*   *   *

Larry dodged a heap of refuse as he hurried down the alleyway. Cristina was in London! Gladbourne said he had seen her at the ball, but his dismissive tone and a casual wave of his hand indicated she'd left. She couldn't be far, though.

She was probably with her parents, traveling in their carriage. Larry would take a few short-cuts through this alley and some other dark paths. That should put him at Cristina's maternal family townhouse just about the time they arrived there. He would find Cristina and win her for himself once and for all.

If she didn't mind the stench of the sludge he had just run through and splashed all over his trousers. What the deuced nastiness was dumped behind these houses, anyway? He paused to do what he could to remove it.

A sound up ahead startled him. In the darkness he could see nothing, but he definitely heard footsteps approaching. Surely no one but a criminal could be lurking in such a place as this. He ducked into the little gap between a wall and a stack of old crates that must have been used to move furniture and hadn't yet been taken away. Something whiskered jumped onto his shoulder and scurried down his arm.

Oh, but he hoped Cristina realized what he was putting himself through on her behalf! Only true love would make a man ruin his boots and let rodents run over his superfine. For Cristina, though, he'd do all this and more.

He did not especially wish to tangle with footpads,

though, so he stayed hidden as the footsteps trotted closer. They beat a quick cadence, but the sound was light and delicate. Surely a man would have clomped along much more loudly. Was this a child? Larry was perplexed. Who would let their child come along this dirty passage, and in the dark of night?

Only a child in very dire circumstance would be here at this hour. As a gentleman, he could not stand idly by. He had to offer assistance.

Still shuddering from the recent run-in with the rodent, he drew a deep breath and stepped out of hiding just as the footsteps passed his spot.

"I say, may I offer assistance?" he asked chivalrously.

He was immediately rewarded with a swift kick to the family jewels. As he doubled over, an elbow jabbed him between the shoulders. He went down into more of the sludge.

"What the bloody hell...?" he growled, crawling backward to avoid another onslaught.

"Stay away from me!" a female voice hissed at him. "I won't hesitate to defend myself."

"As I'm painfully aware, but—"

On hands and knees in the sludge he glanced up to see her. The sight and the voice all snapped together and at once he recognized his attacker. Despite the searing pain still coursing through him and the piles of trash around them, she was the most beautiful thing he'd ever seen. She was already turning to run away from him, though, so he called her name quickly.

"Cristina!"

She must have recognized his voice despite the temporary falsetto. Instantly, she skidded to a halt and turned wide, terrified eyes on him.

"Larry?"

He staggered to his feet, gritting his teeth and pretending all was well with his person. "Yes, it's me. But what the devil are you doing in this place?"

"Me? What about you?" she responded. "Why aren't you back there making passionate love to Miss Maitland, since you're so keen to marry her?"

"Marry her? I don't want to marry her. Didn't you get my letter?"

"Of course I got your stupid letter!"

"So you understand what I did."

"I understand my head was full of cotton to ever think I cared about you," she said.

This statement hurt far worse than anything her feet or elbows could ever do to him.

"But Cristina... all the things that we shared..."

"Were obviously nothing but trifles to you, Laurence Garville. I should never have been such a fool to believe them."

"Of course you should have!"

"Should have what, been a fool? Yes, it was all very convenient for you, wasn't it."

"No! By God, it wasn't convenient at all." *That much was the God's truth.*

"Oh, so now I've been nothing but a nuisance?"

"Cristina, no... that isn't what I meant at all."

"Don't use my name like that."

"Then how should I use it?"

"You shouldn't. Miss Alvarez del Reyes will suffice.

"But Cristina—"

"Miss Alvarez del Reyes!"

"That's ridiculous. After all that we've meant to each other, all that we've planned for our future—"

She harrumphed with finality. "My future never included Miss Maitland. Apparently yours does."

"What? I explained all that in my letter."

"Clearly you missed a few details. For instance, the fact that you still intend to marry her!"

"But I don't intend to marry her!"

"So you were lying when you throttled your cousin and insisted he give her up so she could marry you?"

"When I... egads, you saw that?" He cringed. Indeed, if Cristina had witnessed some of his recent encounter, no wonder she was confused about his intentions.

"I could hardly miss it," she snapped at him. "You were making such a spectacle of yourself."

"But that was before Gladbourne told me he had met you! Did you eavesdrop on *that* part of the conversation?"

"I saw very little conversation. Did you have any? Or did you go directly from violence toward your cousin to groping Miss Maitland?"

"Honestly, there was no groping. Miss Maitland is like my sister!"

"Then you come from a very peculiar family, sir."

"Well, that much is true, I suppose, but Cristina, please. You misunderstood what you saw, and apparently you left before things got sorted."

"I'm a lady, Mr. Garville. I do not stay to watch while people get... sorted."

"No, let me explain. I only argued with Gladbourne because I believed—wait, someone's coming!"

And sure enough, his plaintive explanation was interrupted. At the far end of the alleyway a carriage pulled up to a stop on the street. He couldn't make out the crest on the door, but he could see the dark forms of two gentlemen climb out from it.

He could hear their words, too, although the meaning was lost. The men spoke in loud, angry Spanish.

"It's Papá!" Cristina exclaimed.

"Excellent," Larry said. "I can finally meet the man face

to face and declare my intentions."

"But I told you, my father does not approve of our match," she insisted, a wild look coming over her pretty face. "He's got someone else in mind for me."

Fury like he'd never felt before welled up in Larry. "Who?"

"Him," Cristina said, pointing down the lane as the two men began walking toward them. "Don Bernardo Miguel Garcia de la Vaca."

Larry couldn't see him clearly. All he knew was the man was tall, well-formed, and spoke Cristina's native tongue with dark, sultry tones. He probably had chiseled features and flashing, dark eyes, as well. Larry hated him in an instant.

"Do you want to marry him?" he asked, his chest too tight to breathe as he waited for Cristina's reply.

She took her sweet time in giving it, too. Finally, though, she spoke softly. "No."

Oxygen rushed back in to his lungs and he grabbed Cristina's hand. He gave her a quick smile and she returned one, just a little. It was more than enough to make Larry's soul come alive and wipe away any worry for consequences.

"Come on then," he offered.

She went willingly with him as he took off running.

Chapter 4

Cristina couldn't possibly run another step. She was gasping for breath and her thin slippers—she'd been at a ball, after all—offered no protection for her tender feet. The delicate silk was ragged and ruined. Her toes had gone numb some time ago as the night air was chilly and damp.

"We have to rest," she wheezed, tugging at Larry's hand.

"Here," he said, trotting them up to an ancient iron gate. "You'll be safe in here."

She hardly thought she was in any actual danger from her own father, but it was reassuring to know that Larry could be so determined to keep her for himself. A wiser young woman might look at the past weeks and determine that Larry was not quite right in the upper story, but she was not feeling particularly wise right now. She was dizzy and breathless and tingling with electricity where his hand pressed her arm.

The gate squeaked and creaked in protest, but Larry swung it open for them. She glanced up and down the dark streets behind them, expecting to see her father's carriage at any moment, but it seemed they had somehow alluded him. Larry slipped through the gate and she followed. Wherever they were, Larry seemed sure they were out of harm's way. She could catch her breath and relax. She found a stone bench and dropped onto it, panting and thankful to be in this place.

At least, she was thankful until she glanced up and discovered herself face to face with doom.

She screamed, shattering the night with her terror. A huge avenging angel with sword drawn and wings flared loomed over her, ready to bring retribution for her wild and wayward behavior. She dove behind Larry for protection. At any moment the creature would lop off his head, and then hers would be next.

But Larry just laughed as she cowered in fear. Laughing was quite a skill for a man who'd just been separated from his head, so she peeked around him to see that the horrible, huge angel had not budged. Nor would it. It was stone, carved and cold and not about to lop anything.

She smacked Larry's arm. "Where have you brought me?"

"The parish burial grounds," he replied, as if this were the most normal place to be right now.

She smacked him again. "A cemetery? It's the middle of the night and you dragged me into a *cemetery*?"

"You said you needed to rest."

"Not permanently!"

"So you'd rather stand on the street and wait for your father to find you?"

"No, he'll take me home and claim this is just one more reason I should marry Don Bernardo instead of you."

"What are his other reasons?"

"The fact that you were dead was fairly high on his list."

"But I'm *not* dead," Larry pointed out. "Maybe he'll approve of me now."

"I think to my father, *pretending* to be dead is actually a little bit worse than truly *being* dead."

"We just have to explain everything to him."

"I still don't understand it all myself. Oh, Larry, what were you thinking?"

"I was thinking that if your father wouldn't allow us to be married, then I didn't want to live," he said. The emotional tremor in his voice nearly broke her heart. "I love you, Cristina."

Her heart leaped at his words, but she forced herself not to respond. There was much more to loving someone than merely speaking the words, after all.

"But you were going to marry Miss Maitland."

He was kneeling before her now. His gaze was so intent that she had to look away but he touched her chin and brought her back to face him. She fell into his eyes the way she always did and was ready to believe anything he might tell her.

"My family had matched me with Netta years ago," he said softly. "She is a dear friend, but she is not you. I never wanted to marry her and she feels the same way. She helped me stage that horrible act, and then I was free. I went to hide at my Aunt Tabitha's house and I sent you that letter. When I didn't hear from you after days and days, I knew you had rejected me."

She touched his face. "Silly man. I thought you were dead! My father took us all to Spain and I never even saw your letter until the very day that I ran away. I came back here to find you."

"And so you did."

"Yes, but you were with Miss Maitland again." She was not about to let him forget this so quickly.

"I told you, she is a good friend! I felt bad for the scandal I'd thrown her into, and when I heard she was being forced to marry my cousin because of it, I knew I'd done wrong by her. As far as I knew, Netta hated Gladbourne. How could I leave her to that sort of fate? I thought you were lost to me forever, so at least I could atone for what I'd done to her."

"But now that I'm here, you'll toss her back to the wolves?"

He gave an odd sort of grin. "To be honest, I'm still a little bit surprised by the turn of events. It seems Netta

75

actually *likes* that particular wolf. And Gladbourne is mad over her. Who knew? My pitiful show of restitution was summarily rejected and their wedding will go on as planned first thing tomorrow morning, in this very church as a matter of fact."

"Let's hope it appears more inviting for them tomorrow." She shuddered.

He ran his hands up and down her arms, attempting to warm her. "Yes, let's hope so. I'll have to admit this is not the most romantic place for me to beg for your hand, once again."

"Indeed," she agreed. "This is a horrible place. But go ahead anyway."

He smiled, beaming at her as he took her hands in his. He opened his mouth to profess his love and speak the words that, once again, would make her melt on the inside. She could hardly wait to hear them.

Sadly, his voice was not the one that broke the silence of the night.

"Who's out there?" someone called.

It was not Papá or Don Bernardo. It was a voice she didn't recognize and it was accompanied by approaching footsteps. Larry leaped to his feet and stood before her, shielding her from whatever danger might be approaching. She felt just a bit sheepish for having been so willing to sacrifice him to the stone angel, but then again, he had put her through weeks of torment.

A man appeared through the shadows. We wore a long banyan over, apparently, his nightshirt and his gray head was adorned with a lopsided night cap. Obviously he had not traveled far to get here.

"What is this, ruffians?" he demanded, coming closer.

"No, sir," Larry assured him. "We were just..." His voice trailed off as it became apparent there really wasn't any reasonable explanation for their presence here just now.

The elderly man squinted at them, his gaze lingering on Larry.

"Lord Gladbourne? Is that you?" he asked.

Cristina had noticed Larry's resemblance to his cousin earlier, and she supposed that to a weak eye in this dim light it might be very easy to mistake one man for the other. She never would, of course, but the man in the nightcap was obviously not in love with either gentleman so he was not quite as discerning. He smiled at Larry and gave her a meaningful wink.

"So, you brought your dearly intended here a bit early, did you?"

Cristina was confused, but the man continued and she slowly put the pieces together.

"Could you not wait for the morning?" The man chuckled. "It's but a few hours more, then all will be official and I'll let you both sign the register."

Clearly this was the local vicar and he thought they were Gladbourne and Miss Maitland! She wasn't sure if she should allow him to continue in his confusion, or admit to the truth. Larry made the decision for her. He, as it seemed, was done with falsehood.

"Mr. Shelford," he said, bowing slightly for the gentleman. "I'm afraid you mistake me for my cousin. I am Laurence Garville, not Lord Gladbourne."

The vicar blinked in surprise, leaning in and squinting as if not sure what to believe.

"Garville? No, Garville is dead. I officiated at the funeral."

Larry winced noticeably. "Er, sorry about that. It seems that funeral was a bit premature."

Mr. Shelford shook his head sadly, obviously not quite grasping Larry's words. "Sad affair it was, too. Suicide, you

77

know. Put a blight on a good family."

"But that's why I came back," Larry tried to explain. "I *will* see things right."

The older man just kept shaking his head and turned doleful eyes on Cristina. "Are you certain you want to marry into this family, miss?"

The question caught her off guard, but it was a fair one. Larry *had* been about to ask her again. She needed to give an answer.

"I do, sir," she replied. "With my whole heart. That's why we came here. We are escaping a man who wishes to carry me away!"

She rather intentionally left out the part about the man being her father. It didn't matter, though. She was of age and able to make her own choices despite what Papá thought was best for her. Papá might choose Don Bernardo, but she was choosing Larry.

"A lady in danger?" Mr. Shelford said with a worried tsk-tsk. "Come with me, then. I'll get you to a safe place, and Mrs. Shelford will find you a warm cup of tea."

Cristina was ready to refuse, feeling that they had imposed on the sleepy gentleman more than enough. It was unfair that they'd interrupted his sleep, and the man's unfortunate misunderstanding of the situation was pricking at her conscience. It would probably be best for all of them if they let him return to his bed while she and Larry sorted out their situation.

Before she could find words to extricate them from this mess, though, another person appeared amongst the tombstones. It was either a very irritated banshee, or it was Mrs. Shelford.

"By the blessed saints above us... what is going on out here, Mr. Shelford?" she called, waving a flickering taper as she moved toward them.

"It's nothing, my dearest," the vicar replied. "Just Lord Gladbourne and his intended being a bit impatient for tomorrow."

The woman wrinkled her already wrinkly brow and peered at them. "Gladbourne? What lies are you listening to, Mr. Shelford? This isn't Gladbourne."

The man questioned his wife and studied Larry's face even as two more sets of footsteps charged up behind them.

"This isn't Gladbourne?" the vicar repeated.

"No," the booming voice of a newcomer declared. "But I am."

* * *

Demme it all, but now Gladbourne had shown up. Larry wished he could be happier to see his cousin, but Gladbourne's fiery expression let him know he hadn't miraculously gained favor in the man's eyes even after he'd so graciously relinquished Netta to him. Netta seemed happy enough to have been relinquished, too. She trailed along behind Gladbourne, clinging to his hand and dubiously eyeing the tombstones and statuary around them.

"I see you found your woman," Gladbourne growled, nodding toward Cristina.

Larry placed his body carefully between her and Gladbourne. "Yes. Yes I did, cousin."

"See?" The vicar's banshee screeched at her husband. "*This* one is Gladbourne. The other must be his cousin, Garville."

Mr. Shelford shook his head, the point of his nightcap flopping in the damp air. "Garville's been gone these many weeks. We laid him to rest, poor soul."

"Well you didn't do a very good job of it," the wife argued. "Seems he's come back."

"Is this true?" Mr. Shelford asked Larry, finally beginning to grasp the situation. "Are you the deceased Mr.

Garville?"

Larry wasn't quite sure how to reply to that, but he did anyway. "I am Mr. Garville, but I've never really been deceased."

"What are you doing here then?" the vicar asked.

"This is Miss del Reyes," Larry said. "We came here to hide because she really is being pursued by someone."

"Who is after her?" Mr. Shelford questioned.

"Papá!" Cristina exclaimed.

It took Larry a moment to realize that she wasn't merely answering the question with fervor, but she was reacting to the fact that her father and that dashed chisel-faced Spaniard had just arrived in the cemetery with them.

Larry swore under his breath and then prayed that all the scuffling of feet and gasps of astonishment might have covered the sound. He already had more than enough things to atone for. Cursing in the churchyard did not need to be added to his account.

"What is going on here?" Cristina's father demanded.

"Papá, I did not mean for you to find me," she said, her voice quivering just a bit.

Larry held her hand to provide comfort. And to inform the Spaniard just where things stood.

"But what are you doing?" her father asked, softening his tone just a bit.

"I am running away," she replied. "With Lord Larry."

"*Que lastima, cara mia,*" her father said, shaking his head. "*El hombre está muerto.*"

Larry knew just enough Spanish to deduce the man's meaning. *The man is dead.* Ah, here was a point Larry could absolutely speak to. So he did, stepping forward and presenting himself to Cristina's father.

"No, sir. I am not dead."

The older man glared at him, raising one thick, dark

eyebrow and measuring Larry from head to foot.
"You are Laurence Garville?" he asked.

"I am sir," Larry declared.

The Spanish gentlemen exchanged wondering glances
and the younger one shrugged. Cristina's father continued.
"So you are not dead. But you are engaged to some
other woman?"

"No sir," Larry was happy to say. "My cousin is
engaged to some other woman, but my affections belong
only to Cristina."

"But Cristina is promised to my countryman, Don
Bernardo Miguel Garcia de la Vaca, son of el
Excelentísimo Señor, el Conte de Palma d'Oro " her father
said.

The chiseled Spaniard bowed slightly as his impressive
name was rattled off. Larry hated everything about the
man. What woman could turn down this dashing Grandee
whose designation took half an hour to pronounce in favor
of a simple heir-apparent with a ruddy courtesy title? And
one who'd been declared dead, at that?

He could only hope the advanced hour, the chill in the
air, and her days of travel had left Cristina somehow
muddled in the brain. Surely if she were fully possessed of
her faculties she would recognize that she deserved far
better than Larry. He knew for a fact that he did not deserve
her.

"No, Papá," she said, squeezing Larry's hand and
leaning into him. "I am promised to Lord Larry."

It was not the most illustrious name, but it was *his*. The
way Cristina uttered it with tenderness and devotion made
him feel as if he were ruler of the whole world. Or at least,
this little corner of it. He would take on every vicar, cousin
or Spaniard on the planet in order to finally make her his
bride.

Susan Gee Heino

Chapter 5

Cristina waited for Papá's explosion. He must be furious with her, running off as she had done. Aside from being dangerous, it was also quite costly to obtain passage for her and her maid on a ship. To cover it, she'd sold a rather expensive necklace that Papá had given her. He would be angry and hurt when he learned of that, no doubt.

Once they made it to London, Cristina and her maid had gone straight to her grandfather's nearly deserted townhouse. As the family was not using it this Season, only a servant or two had been kept to look after it. Not much security for a lady alone, yet it was better than wandering the streets. Which, come to think of it, she'd ended up doing anyway.

It was all very foolish, really, and she should have known Papá would learn of her flight and follow almost immediately. No doubt she'd be subjected to his wrath now, right here in front of everyone. She prayed he wouldn't blame Larry and made trouble for him, or talk of satisfaction and duels.

Papá was an excellent shot. Larry—as evidenced by the fact that he was still here—couldn't even shoot himself. She held her breath, waiting for Papá's response. He was doing that terrifying thing he did with his eyebrow as he glared back and forth between her and Larry.

"So what is it you've promised to do for this Lord Larry?" Papá asked her suspiciously.

She matched his eyebrow smirk with one of her own. "Marry him, of course."

Now his eyes held daggers for Larry. "Is this true? Your intentions for my daughter are respectable?"

"Of course, sir!" Larry replied, not quite as daunted by the eyebrow and daggers as Cristina might have expected. "Everything I've done has been a misguided plan to make her my wife."

Papá sheathed his evil glare and looked Larry over with slightly less malice. "You have the means to provide for my daughter properly, young man? Who are your connections?"

Larry seemed only too happy to wave his breeding for Papá to see. He explained that his father was the second son of an earl, but the elder son who inherited had not produced any male heirs so it was assumed the title and estate would eventually pass on to Larry. He proudly presented Lord Gladbourne as his first cousin on his mother's side, proving that—despite recent uncharacteristic behaviors—he truly was every bit as well bred and connected as Don Bernardo. Papá listened intently and seemed mildly impressed.

"And you believe you are worthy of my daughter?" he asked finally.

Larry shook his head. "No sir. I'm quite certain I am not worthy of her, but I assure you I will spend every day of the rest of my life trying to make myself so."

It was an excellent answer. She fell in love with him all over again. Now, if only Papá would do the same!

It seemed Lord Gladbourne had softened a bit from earlier. His face had displayed nothing less than raw fury when Cristina presented him with Larry's letter. Now, however, he actually spoke up in defense of his cousin.

"Despite recent judgment errors, my cousin is a good man, sir," he said with sincerity. "I am convinced his commitment to your daughter is secure and he will do right. However, if in the future he does ever get any addle-pated notions about shamming his own death again, I will personally see to it that your daughter gets first crack at him."

That seemed perfectly reasonable to Cristina, and Papá apparently agreed. Much to Cristina's surprise, he did not argue or demand further assurances from Larry. Instead, he nodded and turned to Don Bernardo. For the sake of the others, he spoke in English.

"It appears, my friend, that you have lost your intended. Do you wish to take issue with this?"

Don Bernardo bowed to Cristina, his perfectly cultured form still not as appealing to her as Larry's adorable quirks and missteps. She allowed the gracious Spaniard to take her hand as he nodded over it. There had never been any pretense of tender emotion between them, but it still panged her to think she had disappointed him by breaking her pledge.

His warm smile helped ease her conscience.

"I have very much enjoyed our acquaintance, *señorita*, and I do hope that when I am again in your country, you and your Lord Larry will welcome me as a guest into your home."

"Thank you, Don Bernardo," she said to him. "I wish you very well. Of course you will always be considered a dear friend to us."

It was all going surprisingly well and she glanced nervously at Papá. Was he really so willing to accept Larry after he had made it plain to her just last month that he heartily disapproved him? He hadn't even given her reason, just informed her that in his opinion, Lord Larry had done nothing to show he cared deeply for her and would remain true after the first blush of infatuation had worn off.

It was impossible to think anything Larry had done recently would shine him in a more favorable light.

"Papá," she said cautiously. "We truly do want your blessing. I couldn't bear it if you resented me for making this choice. Will you really allow me to marry Lord Larry?"

"*Cara mia*," Papá said. "You have left me little choice. You ran away from your family, you've evaded me and come here alone with this man. By morning, all of London will be speaking of little else. There is nothing I can do to salvage your good name aside from allowing you to marry this man."

Her heart sank. Oh, but this sounded dreadfully like what she had expected. Papá was sadly disappointed in her and he really would resent her forever. If he felt strongly enough, he could ban her from his home forever! Yes, she would end up with Larry, but had she lost her dear family in the process?

"Please, sir," Larry said quickly. "You can't blame Cristina. She was only reacting to the terrible thing I had done. Please don't hold her accountable for my deplorable actions."

"Yes, what you did was deplorable," Papá said, turning his focus onto Larry. "Do you know how my poor child suffered, how she grieved when word came that you had perished, and in such a gruesome manner? I despaired for her! What rational explanation can you give for what you have done?"

Larry stammered a bit. It seemed he could not give any sort of rational explanation. To everyone's surprise, Miss Maitland spoke up and presented one.

"If you please, sir, it wasn't entirely Larry's fault. I had a hand in what happened."

"And you are...?" Papá asked with the hint of another eyebrow stare.

"Netta Maitland. I am the other one Lord Larry was engaged to marry, sir."

Papá nodded as if this confirmed some deep suspicions. "Ah, so you are in love with this Larry."

"No, sir," Miss Maitland said quickly. "Not at all! Oh,

he's a good friend and I assure you he'll make an excellent husband for your daughter, but I never fancied myself in love with him. I am in love with Lord Gladbourne and we are to marry tomorrow."

Lord Gladbourne rather beamed at that pronouncement. Cristina did, too. Hearing from the woman's own lips that she was not in love with Larry was like angel song. Papá didn't seem to enjoy the tune, though.

"If you didn't love the man, why were you engaged to him?"

Miss Maitland seemed decidedly uncomfortable. "I don't know, sir. Our families had been planning it so long, I don't even know when it became official. Once he met your daughter, though, it was clear to us that we couldn't go through with it."

Now Papá's attention was back onto Larry. "And the only thing you could think of was to pretend suicide with a pistol? And an explosion? And a fire?"

Larry shrugged like a sheepish child. "Love leads us to do desperate things, sir."

Lord Gladbourne grumbled under his breath. "You mean, *stupid* things."

Miss Maitland nudged him with her elbow.

Papa folded his arms across his chest and gave Larry one last, lingering look. "How will I know you won't continue to do stupid things?"

This time Larry had an answer. "Because, sir. Love also leads us to become better men than we were. I will never run from my troubles or resort to deception again. I will only ever run *toward* Cristina, with honesty and devotion . I promise you that."

Mr. Shelford and his wife had been watching the banter with interest. At this point Mrs. Shelford sniffled and pulled a handkerchief from her wrapper to dab at her eyes. The vicar smiled and declared Larry's pronouncement the very epitome of Godly principle and grace. Cristina hoped Papá would not argue.

He didn't. "Well said, sir. Now I suggest we all get in from the night air. We have much to arrange, and I believe these other young people have a very big day tomorrow."

"We'd love you and your daughter to attend," Miss Maitland said quickly. "And the breakfast directly after. We will all be family, as it appears."

"So it appears," Papá said. "*Por Dios.*"

They said good-night to the Shelford's and began to leave the burial yard. Lord Gladbourne chuckled under his breath and shook his head at his cousin.

"Dash it all, Larry. You abandoned poor Netta, shot yourself in the head, and burned yourself up on a boat, all in the hope of avoiding a marriage. And now marriage is what you *want*?"

Larry rested his hand over Cristina's as he led her through the iron gate. His eyes met hers and he smiled. "It's what I wanted all along. My whole scheme was to end up married to you, Cristina Maria Magdalena Alvarez del Reyes."

Her heart was so full she thought it might burst into a thousand bright colors. Papá very politely ignored them so she squeezed Larry's arm and snuggled up tightly against him. From this point onwards, she determined to forget all about his deception and her grief, the anger and the jealousy. She would concentrate only on their happy future.

Yes, Larry did plot and scheme, but it was all done for love of her. She would always treasure that. He grinned as she whispered into his ear.

"And what an elegant scheme it was, sir. I can hardly wait to see what you will plan for us next."

The Ghostly Goal of Scary Lord Larry

A Regency Ghost Story

by Susan Gee Heino

Dedication

To Joylyn.
Because you like scary ghosts and happy endings, too.

Chapter 1

Surrey, England, October 1817

The dark bedroom held the musty, vacant feel of having been closed up too long. Amelie D'Arnaud shifted her pillows and tried to make herself comfortable, but it was no use. She simply couldn't get settled.

The heavy bed curtains hung over her like dense, dusty specters and she shut her eyes, trying to ignore them. But now her ears plagued her. What was that sound from the hallway? Where those footsteps in the empty rooms up above? Was that a draft from the window, or had something brushed her cheek? Indeed, her mind was awhirl with terrifying possibilities.

It was all silliness, of course. She should not have let her companions fill her head with such nonsense tonight after dinner. Cristina Garville and her husband, Larry, had merely been entertaining their guests when they told stories of resident ghosts and dark apparitions haunting the labyrinth of corridors and rooms here at Cliffside Manor. Surely none of it was in anyway real.

After all, there were no such things as ghosts; everyone knew that. Well, perhaps everyone but dotty old Aunt Tabitha. She was enthralled with the stories, adding her own recollections of strange goings-on from days gone by.

At the time, surrounded by friends in the bright lamplight of the cozy drawing room, Amelie had laughed at the fanciful tales. It never dawned on her that her mind would be run away with such twaddle once the lamps were doused and everyone retired to their beds. Now here she was wishing the group had talked of puppies and kittens instead of restless spirits and ghouls.

A distinct thump just outside her door caused her to jump. She pressed her hand over her mouth to keep from crying aloud. What in heaven's name could that have been?

Well, it certainly couldn't have been a ghost. There weren't any of those. She repeated that over and over in her mind.

Yet there it was again, a ghostly, horrible thump.

She pulled the covers over her head and waited. Was it coming to get her? Was some ghastly phantom on its way from the underworld to collect her soul even now? Well, if so, the mere fabric of a blanket or two would hardly protect her. She needed a weapon.

This particular room was woefully short of those, however. As she slipped out of bed and pulled on her dressing gown, she scanned her surroundings for anything that might be of use in her situation. She found nothing even remotely weapon-like, which would generally be a good thing, but with spooks at the door and poltergeists in the walls, a blunderbuss or a handy mace would be a comfort just now.

Lacking any of those, she was forced to consider the next best thing. On the table near the bed she had noticed a stack of books. One of them was a Bible. Not only would that be a holy implement to ward off evil, but it was of a good size, and heavy. Any otherworldly being would surely think twice before approaching her to have its non-corporeal form scattered by a swiping blow from that sacred tome.

A sliver of moonlight beamed through a gap in the drapes. There was just enough light to find the table. Aha, here were the books. She fumbled with them, grabbing up the largest and most religiously weapon-like one of the bunch. Now she was prepared to do battle.

Slippers on her feet and her wrapper pulled tight, she tip-toed to the door and opened it slowly. A quick glance up and down the corridor showed it to be empty. Perhaps she had imagined everything. But no, a muffled noise caught her attention. This was more than a thump; it was a thud, and it came from behind a door at the end of the corridor.

A door to a room that she knew was unoccupied.

Clutching the Bible, she slipped into the corridor. The house was full of guests, but she knew which room each and every one of them was in. At the end nearest the staircase, there were rooms for the guests of honor, Lord and Lady Gladbourne. Across from them was Lady Gladbourne's father, then next to that a room for Aunt Tabitha. Next to her room was Miss Poppy Fairwell—whom Amelie could certainly do without—and at the other end of the corridor were rooms for the master and his lady, Mr. Larry Garville—whom they all lovingly called Lord Larry, since he was in line to inherit some distant title—and Amelie's dear friend, the newly-web Mrs. Cristina Garville.

The room across from theirs—the room where the noise originated—was not assigned. No one should be there. No one should be making thumps or thuds or any sort of noise in that room.

Yet someone was.

Amelie crept along the dark corridor, moving silently toward that door. Everyone in the household was sleeping and her ears perked for the tiniest sound. The unoccupied room seemed to have gone completely still, but wait... another sound.

Not from within that room, though. This sound came from behind her. Footsteps!

She whirled around, scanning the shadows of the long corridor behind her. Was she being followed? The footsteps stopped.

But now, a deep, heavy sigh. Heavens! Had she made that sound? No. Someone else had. Someone unseen was sighing from somewhere along this corridor. The low whisper of breath was unmistakable.

So why could she not see this person? Her eyes had become well accustomed to the dark. Were the shadowy recesses of the doorways so deep that a person could hide there unseen, even as she gazed intently for them?

And there... a floorboard creaked. A floorboard in the very center of the corridor. A floorboard that could only have been bent by a passing foot. Yet no foot, no body, no person could be seen there at all. Amelie was being approached by someone invisible!

Fear tightened her chest, her own breath stolen by terror even as her ears detected another unmistakable sigh—this one closer than the last. She felt a cold puff of air whoosh over her. And now another floorboard, also closer than the last. Some strange phantom was drawing nearer, nearer to her in this dark, lonely corridor and all she had to defend herself was a book.

Shaking and wild, she reacted on instinct. The door latch lifted easily and she swung the door open to the empty room just in front of her. She leaped inside, shutting the door tight behind her and pressing her back against it. Please, God, let her have enough strength to block out whatever horror was on the outside of that door.

But that was not her only concern. It only took half a second to realize things were not entirely peaceful *inside* of this door, either. She had retreated into this room to be alone, and she had failed. This room, apparently, was not as unoccupied as she had expected.

In fact, it was very much occupied.

And the occupier was *naked*.

"Miss D'Arnaud?" he said.

She was too busy gawking to respond.

Naked! Oh, but by the saints and apostles, she'd walked in on Mr. Roland Bentley and he was *naked*!

"Can I help you with something?" he asked.

"I... er, but you... that is, you're—"

"Yes, I'm here now," he said, grabbing up a towel from the wash stand nearby and strategically covering himself. At least, the most important parts of himself. "I didn't think I could attend Lord Larry's house party so I sent my regrets, but at the last minute my plans changed so I set out."

"Oh. I see." And indeed she did. Far, far too much.

"I rained," he said simply. "That is, I was delayed by the weather. The roads were a sea of mud and I arrived quite a mess."

The man was certainly not a mess now. "How fortunate that you got here at all."

"Yes, it is," he agreed. "As it was so late, I was lucky to rouse a servant to let me in. I hoped not to wake anyone. I'm sorry that I did, obviously."

"What? Oh, no, you didn't wake anyone."

He frowned. She hardly noticed it. "Then why are you here?"

"Here? Oh, my heavens, I nearly forgot. There is a moaning specter in the hallway!"

"A what?"

"Well, sighing, really; not moaning. And knocking about making quite a racket, too. That is what woke me, I'm afraid. I had no idea you were in here."

"You thought I was a specter?"

"No, I thought you were no one," she tried to explain, not really sure where to focus her eyes. "The specter was coming after me in the corridor, so I ducked in here to escape."

Finally he seemed suitably alarmed. "Someone was chasing you?"

He made as if to rush toward her, but apparently recalled his current natural state and paused. She barely held back a giggle as the towel slipped and he was forced to quickly readjust it.

"Er, perhaps you could turn your back for a moment, Miss D'Arnaud? I would rather like to gird my loins before doing battle with your pursuer."

Oh, but she ought not be laughing at the poor man just now. She turned quickly, her face flaming, and stared at the door. A quick scrabble of fabric behind her and the sounds of his hurried motions indicated he had located his trousers and was pulling them on.

My, but they must be gliding over his manly calves, brushing past muscular thighs. And after that... why, they would be sliding up to encompass his firm backside, and then... heavens, but just the sound of the man getting dressed filled her with wild imaginings.

It was always like this with him. She was the most delicate and proper of ladies, until Roland Bentley was around. Then her mind abandoned all pretense of respectability and ran away with horrible, delightful fantasies. Now to have walked in on him like this... it was doubtful she would ever recover.

But she had to, and quickly. Even if she cast herself out of his room right this moment, ran down the hall and dove back into her own bed, her misery would hardly be over. Dawn would break, the sun would rise, and another day would be upon them. Then she would have to face him.

They were guests here in the same house now, after all. They'd be tripping over each other tomorrow. She could not avoid him, and he could not avoid her. If they even attempted it, people would notice—and wonder at it. Her stomach knotted and twisted as she stared at the door and pictured everything he was doing behind her.

This was truly the most shocking, mortifying, delicious moment of her life.

"There now," he said finally, indicating he was appropriately clothed. "Who must I murder?"

She turned slowly back to him. Thankfully, he was trousered, and a clean linen shirt covered the rest of him. His eyes... oh, but the fire that burned in Roland Bentley's dark eyes was just as indecent as ever.

"Murder? No need for that, sir," she informed. "Whoever it is, is already dead."

Susan Gee Heino

Chapter 2

"Already dead?" Roland asked.

As usual, Miss D'Arnaud put him off guard and set his mind reeling. He could hardly form words in her presence, let alone make sense of any. Who could she be running from and was someone here at Cliffside Manor really dead? Surely that wouldn't make for a very amusing house party.

But the thought that she might be in danger cleared the fog from his brain and let it function freely. Miss D'Arnaud was in peril and she'd come to him for protection! He reached past her for the door handle. Whoever was out there, he'd make short work of them.

"I'll see to this villain," he announced.

She stopped his hand. "No... I doubt that you will."

Perhaps he ought to get a bit more information before throwing himself into harm's way. "Is your attacker armed, Miss D'Arnaud?"

"Not that I know of. Can bodiless spirits carry weapons?"

"Er... bodiless spirits?"

"That's what I was running from!" She moved away from him, her eyes bright and the incredible story spilling out quickly. "I heard noises from the hallway and left my room to see what they were. But I found nothing! Still, the noises persisted, following me up the corridor. I looked and I looked, but no one was there."

"No one? Who was making the noises, then?"

"It has to be a ghost!"

"A ghost? You do realize how ridiculous that sounds."

"It did not sound ridiculous when it was breathing on me, chasing me."

"And what is this, did you think to fend it off with a... with a Bible?"

"I did not travel here with a full arsenal of implements for battling the dead."

"It would seem that particular book might be more useful for the living."

Her wide eyes narrowed and she pursed her pink lips at him. "Are you making fun of me?"

"You have to admit, running from phantoms does sound a little ridiculous."

"So I'm ridiculous? Well, maybe I am. I, however, do not go traipsing about naked in the middle of the night!"

"I was not the one traipsing, Miss D'Arnaud. I was in the privacy of my own room, changing out of wet traveling clothes and into a dry nightshirt. I had intended to do so without any audience at all—human *or* ghost."

"So you *do* believe there is a ghost!"

"Of course I don't believe there's a ghost. What the devil were you really doing prowling around at this hour?"

"Prowling? You make it sound as if I made my way in here on purpose."

"No, I didn't mean that—"

"You meant that I am being foolish. Well, sir, I supposed I can't argue with that. I am being foolish to think I can enlist your help in this matter."

Now he'd done it. Any trace of fear was gone from her eyes and was replaced by a flash of pure anger. He should have been much, much more careful with his words, and he knew it.

"Amelie, please—" He was only to be cut off by the murderous look she gave him.

"*Amelie*, is it?" she queried, drawing her words out with deadly precision. "It's been quite a good while since we were onto first names. I'm surprised you remember it. But no matter. I should not be here, inflicting my ridiculous foolishness on you, sir. Forgive me interrupting your *toilette* for something so inane as saving my life."

"I'm sorry, but—"

She was not listening to him. Dismissing his protest with the wave of her delicate hand, she pushed past him and pulled open the door. Apparently whatever was out there no longer offended her nearly as much as he had. Once again he had disappointed her, and once again she merely put her chin up in the air and marched away from him.

"Good night, Mr. Bentley. Perhaps in the morning we can think of this as nothing more than a bad dream. That's what I've been doing for years where you are concerned."

Without even a backward glance, she turned, clutched her Bible before her as a shield, and padded softly up the corridor. Of course he couldn't very well call after her or risk waking other house guests and bringing on a wave of questions and scandal, but he'd be damned if he was going to leave the woman out there unattended. She may no longer prefer his company, but he could at least watch over to make certain she arrived safely at her room.

Besides, he couldn't help but be just a bit interested in knowing which of these doors along the corridor were hers. Not that it mattered to him, of course. His right to have interest in Miss D'Arnaud's sleeping arrangements evaporated the day he broke off their engagement. That had been the day after he learned that his father had squandered the family fortune and leapt off the tallest tower of what had once been a proud castle, home to generations of Bentley family ancestors.

Just as Roland's life was, the castle existed as nothing more than ruins and would have been a poor offering for a beautiful young wife. Amelie deserved so much more than poverty and his father's tainted legacy. Roland had been doing her a kindness to release her from their betrothal. It had nearly killed him, but clearly she'd not suffered permanent damage from it.

He tried to take solace from that, but he was just a little bit too selfish to find any comfort there. He had loved Amelie D'Arnaud and wanted her for himself. That had not changed, no matter how much his prospects in life had.

He stood guard in the corridor, watching over her as she silently opened the door to her chamber. It appeared that she spared one last glance in his direction, but with the shadows and dim light he could have been imagining. He might have merely seen what he wanted to see. The truth was, she gave no indication of wasting any further time on thoughts of him or his person.

Her door clicked shut behind her. The corridor was silent; there was no sign of anything that might have upset her and caused her to retreat into his room. What on earth had spooked the woman? Surely she didn't really believe in ghosts.

He waited there, peering up and down, into the darkness. Had someone else been here with her? What was she doing stalking the hallway at this hour, anyway? Roland had tried to be quiet, to settle into his room without waking anyone. Had it been his bumbling about that she'd heard and mistaken for a spirit?

There was no sign of anything else. Finally, he could do nothing but go back inside his room, close the door, and assume that Miss D'Arnaud's sleepy brain had imagined much more than just the sounds of a weary traveler arriving at night. With any luck, she'd do as she said. She'd wake up tomorrow and believe all of this to be nothing more than a bad dream. Yes, that would be best, even if his wavering self-confidence would much rather picture her tossing and turning all night, tormented by thoughts of *him*.

And she certainly had seen more than enough of him to fill her thoughts. By God, he'd been fully stripped down when the woman walked in! It was the most devastating thing to realize that she'd hardly seemed affected. Dash it all, but he'd stood before her in nothing more than a bit of linen and she'd barely batted an eye. It was almost as if she encountered naked men every night of the week.

Damn it, but that thought struck him like a plank on the side of the head. Perhaps he wasn't the first man she'd encountered that way. Hellfire. Perhaps the woman had recovered from his abandonment quite well; surely there would be plenty of men happy to take his place in her affections. Perhaps she had accepted one of them. Or more.

In fact... perhaps that was her *real* reason for wandering the hallway tonight. By God, who else was a guest at this house party? She could have a lover among the crowd and been on her way to see him! Indeed, she could very well have simply let herself into the wrong room. That story of fearing a ghost might have been nothing more than a spur-of-the-moment excuse she made up to hide her indiscretion.

Oh, he was furious at the thought of it. Try as he might to convince himself it was outlandish, the more believable it was. Far more believable than ghost stories, in fact. Amelie D'Arnaud was a beautiful woman. She was no longer a timid schoolgirl, either. She was an adult, fully capable of engaging in adult activity. Was that what she had really been up to? Had she taken a wrong turn on her way to a secret tryst?

Damn it all, but he would have much rather believed the ghost story. He'd stand a better chance of getting any sleep tonight if that was all he had to worry over. To think that Amelie might have a living, flesh-and-blood lover somewhere in this house, well, that was more soul-sucking than any malicious specter could ever be.

Cursing, Roland put out the lamp and climbed into a

cold, lonely bed. Minutes ticked by as he stared into darkness, begging sleep to take him. He had finally begun to calm the tumult in his brain when an odd sound from the corridor startled him. What was it? He listened.

The floor creaked. Yes, that was the unmistakable sound of a creaking floor. Old houses did that. He tried not to be concerned.

But there was another... and another. Not just random creaks, but footsteps. The cadence was undeniable. Someone was passing his doorway, moving up the corridor toward Miss D'Arnaud's room!

He hoped the sounds would continue on. Perhaps it was someone headed down to the kitchens in search of a late-night meal. But no; the footsteps paused, then he heard the distinctive squeak of a hinge. A door opened silently.

He couldn't help himself. Instantly, he was out of bed and dashing to his own door. He would see Miss D'Arnaud's secret lover. He would know who had won her affections and was allowed access to her boudoir.

But the corridor was empty. Every door was shut tight, no sign of movement anywhere. He scanned up and down, glaring at every shadow, every recess. Nothing.

He watched Miss D'Arnaud's door closely. There was no sound, no hinge, no motion, not anything to indicate someone had just entered there. Apparently Roland had been too slow. The man was inside already and he'd missed seeing him. He cursed himself silently.

But then there was that noise again. The floorboard creaked, and the hinge squeaked again. Yet his eyes detected no one! By God, he was hearing sound, yet seeing nothing.

He blinked in amazement, but the sound faded into the night. The corridor was quiet again. For the longest time he stood there, but nothing happened. It was as if he had imagined all of it.

Had he? Perhaps. He was dead tired after his laborious journey, after all. It had been a shock to find Miss D'Arnaud in his room; perhaps that had set his mind on flights of fancy. This would not be the first time her presence had done that to him.

He had to get a hold of himself. Ghosts were not real, and whatever Miss D'Arnaud was up to in the night, it was none of his business. Somehow he had to simply put it all from his mind and get some rest. God knew he needed it.

He began to shut his door, but his eye caught on the doorway across from him. The footsteps—if they had been real—would have originated there. Just who was that room's occupant? It would certainly be interesting in the morning to discover who might have been wandering the halls toward Miss D'Arnaud's bedroom.

Chapter 3

Amelie D'Arnaud enjoyed the tasty cakes set out with a most excellent breakfast. It was almost enough to restore her after a long, sleepless night. It was especially good that Mr. Bentley had not yet appeared to spoil her appetite; she could chew in peace, so far. Their hostess, Mrs. Cristina Garville, kept the mood at table bright and cheerful. Thankfully, she was oblivious to the dark circles under Amelie's eyes.

"Since the day appears so sunny and bright," Cristina was saying, "I thought perhaps we might all enjoy a picnic by the lake after the men have returned from shooting."

Miss Poppy Fairwell, sitting across from Amelie, sipped at her tea and chirped happily. "Is that what they are doing today? I wondered where they were. It's so unlike gentlemen to let a breakfast go undevoured."

And it is so unlike you to let any gentleman go undevoured, Amelie thought. But it was ungenerous so she kept it to herself. Poppy Fairwell was an empty-headed twit who wouldn't give a fig for what Amelie thought of her, anyway.

"I don't believe the shooting has started," Cristina informed. "My husband went out early to see to the men getting things ready for them. The other two gentlemen should be here presently."

"Shooting seems such a dangerous pastime," Aunt Tabitha declared as she spooned jam onto her plate. "All those guns... one just never knows what terrible things might happen."

Amelie traded glances with Cristina. Indeed, they both knew Aunt Tabitha's penchant to worry. They also both knew it would be pointless to argue.

Tabitha Dibbley was not truly Amelie's aunt, but she was some sort of relation to Lord Larry Garville. Amelie's family had been close to the Garvilles, so the old woman was very much like an auntie to her, as well. Years ago there'd been an Uncle Erwin Dibbley to go with her, but he had died tragically in an accident that may or may not have been suspicious.

Left alone with no children of her own, Aunt Tabitha had doted on those close to her. She had taken a particular liking to Larry Garville and actually lived here with his family for a time. Ever since the poor woman lost her husband she had refused to stay in her own home. For years now she'd shuffled between friends and relations, fretting and fussing no matter where she was. Larry and Cristina were very gracious to invite her to come stay with them now.

"Lord Larry has instructed his men to use the utmost caution in everything," Cristina assured the older woman, patient as a saint. "But of course we can remind them to take care when the do pop in for a bite before heading out to the fields."

As if she conjured them, two men appeared in the doorway now. Neither of them was Roland Bentley. They were other guests, Lord Larry's cousin from his mother's side, Lord Gladbourne, and his lordship's father-in-law, Mr. Maitland. They paused in the doorway, allowing Lord Gladbourne's wife to enter ahead of them.

"Ah, good morning, Netta," Cristina greeted.

The two women had been fast friends—once the matter of which one of them was going to marry Lord Larry got settled. Amelie herself had grown quite fond of Lady Gladbourne and, if not for the fact that Roland Bentley might appear at any moment, the company this morning would have been delightful.

"I'm sorry to be such a dawdler," Lady Gladbourne said, bustling into the room and bringing a ray of sunshine along with her.

It was almost sickening, in fact, how radiant the woman was. Cristina, as well. Both women had married the loves of their lives and it was excruciatingly obvious how happy they were. The glow almost blinded, in fact.

Amelie reminded herself that she was glad for them, but of course she was slightly more envious than glad. She wished she could convince herself she didn't hold to silly, romantic notions, but of course she did. Her reaction to Roland last night had been ample proof of that.

Drat the man! What could he be thinking, to attend the same house party where he must have known she would be? Perhaps he wasn't the least bit put off by being around her, but he certainly had to realize their close proximity would be somewhat uncomfortable. And how close their proximity had been last night! Good heavens, she felt her face flaming at the mere thought of it.

Thankfully, no one seemed to notice. Lady Gladbourne was busily complimenting Cristina on the comforts of her home, Lord Gladbourne was tolerating a flourish of boot-licking from the socially optimistic Miss Fairwell, while Mr. Maitland had been pulled into Aunt Tabitha's worrisome orbit and was being forced to reassure her repeatedly. For ten whole minutes Amelie was able to safely hide her flushed cheeks as she struggled valiantly to push thoughts of Roland out of her head and some sort of food into her mouth.

She should have known it was too good to last.

"No, it is no use, Mr. Maitland," Aunt Tabitha protested. "You cannot convince me that I am very well today, despite how you claim that I look. I'm quite disheveled."

"You look lovely, as always," the gentleman insisted.

Cristina, ever the excellent hostess, leaped into the conversation to add reassurance. "I'm always in envy of your complexion, Aunt Tabitha. And is this a new shawl you are wearing?"

"Oh, this? No, it's nearly an old rag," Aunt Tabitha said.

"Well, I like it very much," Cristina praised. "It is the perfect shade for the beautiful brooch you always wear. But... I see you're not wearing it today."

Which, Amelie had to note, was very odd. Aunt Tabitha always wore the little gold brooch with the cluster of pearls. It was very precious to her, a gift from her dearly departed Erwin.

"Perhaps I mislaid it," Aunt Tabitha replied with remarkable disinterest. "But no matter. I needed a change, for all the good that it's done. I still look like a weary old woman."

"You are the very picture of grace and vitality, ma'am," Mr. Maitland said, his own cheeks going quite rosy, although that was likely caused by more than just a phlegmatic nature.

Mr. Maitland drank. A lot. It was quite obvious, even from the first day he and his party arrived here. The only one of the group who did not seem to know how obvious it was, was Mr. Maitland himself. He carried himself as if the drink was a very big secret. The rest of the group humored him out of respect.

"Did you not sleep well again, Aunt Tabitha?" Lady Gladbourne asked sweetly.

"No, and I find it unfathomable how the rest of you could so much as shut your eyes over night."

"But the house is quite comfortable," her ladyship insisted with some measure of passion. "Surely if you have need of anything at all, Mrs. Garville will see to it."

Aunt Tabitha sighed dramatically. "Oh, no doubt she might try, but there's just nothing to be done when such things are afoot."

"Such things?" Cristina asked.

"Oh, you know, dear. The things that happen in the night. The unexplainable things."

Cristina looked puzzled, Lady Gladbourne glanced at her husband, and Amelie stared down at her plate of breakfast. Aunt Tabitha had heard unexplainable things in the night! Had she overheard Amelie invading the room of a gentleman? This would be scandal, indeed.

Their hostess, however, simply gave the older woman a patronizing smile. "Now, now, Aunt Tabitha. You aren't talking of your ghosts again, are you?"

"Of course I am!" Aunt Tabitha replied firmly. "I have warned you all that dark spirits prowl this house at night, my dear, and you would do well to believe me. I cannot say yet what they intend for us."

Cristina did not seem the least bit concerned with Tabitha's warning, however. "Of course we've all heard the stories, Aunt Tabitha. But that's all they are. Surely if we really had ghosts here at Cliffside Manor, I would have encountered one of them by now."

Tabitha simply shrugged and offered an ominous explanation. "It could simply be that they haven't decided to come for you yet."

Cristina laughed at the thought, and Lady Gladbourne seemed equally unconcerned, but Amelie's smile lacked the sincerity of theirs. What had she experienced in the hallway last night? Why on earth would a resident phantom ignore the others and torment her? Even now, in bright daylight surrounded by everyone, the cold chill of terror tried to creep up Amelie's spine. She could still hear those ghostly footsteps behind her, the feel of hollow eyes on her, fully present, yet completely unseen.

113

No matter how she might try to convince herself otherwise, Aunt Tabitha's reports of ghosts could not go unheard. Something prowled the halls of Cliffside Manor. Something that was tangible and terrifying enough to send Amelie rushing into Roland Bentley's private room in the middle of the night.

"Amelie, what do you think of it?"

She snapped to awareness. Cristina was speaking to her, asking a question. Amelie had to sheepishly beg her to repeat it.

"Aunt Tabitha's ghosts," the hostess said cheerfully. "Quite frightful, indeed. What do you think of it all?"

Amelie was at a loss. Of course while she would hate to discredit Aunt Tabitha, she could hardly admit what she'd seen with her own eyes. Or rather, *not* seen. It would sound very mad. Roland had called her ridiculous, after all. How could she answer this question? She was at a loss.

"I'm afraid I hardly know what to think," she said finally. "One hears stories like these all the time from every corner of life. Surely there must be some truth if so many people are claiming similar experiences."

"So you believe it is possible?" Lady Gladbourne said, not quite calling Amelie ridiculous, but indicating that she thought as much with her expression.

Aunt Tabitha, however, beamed. "Ah, this one is a sensible miss. She knows the truth of the matter, I daresay."

Everyone had turned to Amelie, waiting for her to reply. Heavens, but what could she say? She must either insult Aunt Tabitha or reveal what she knew and let her friends think her a cotton-headed hysteric. Worse, the more she thought of her fright in the corridor last night, the more she was reminded of her even worse horror walking in on Mr. Bentley! There went those flames in her cheeks again. No no no... she had to change the subject, somehow.

"And just what fascinating matter is Miss D'Arnaud privy to the truth of?"

It was a voice from the doorway; Lord Larry's, as a matter of fact. Indeed, Amelie had wanted something to save her from that discussion, but this was not it. Strolling into the room with Lord Larry was a fully clothed, breathtakingly handsome Roland Bentley.

"What a surprise! It seems Mr. Bentley has joined us," Cristina exclaimed, tipping her head so her husband could place a kiss on her cheek in greeting.

"He has indeed," Lord Larry replied. "Not sure if I mentioned that I invited him, but he's here now and I'm happy for it. We ran into each other in the hallway first thing this morning."

Roland Bentley nodded in deference to the guests. His coat still showed vague signs of the weather he must have faced on his journey, but a fresh cravat was tied in an elegant knot at his throat. He seemed as well-rested and ready for action as if he'd been settled here for days instead of battling muddy roads and being accosted by young women all night. Amelie was just the tiniest bit miffed at how unruffled the man appeared, considering the clamor of nerves and pounding blood inside her at the moment.

"A most convenient happenstance that our host emerged from his room this morning just as I exited mine," he said casually. "Good fortune that our doors should be just across the hall from each other, I suppose. We were well met, so I accompanied him to check preparations for our outing."

"I had no idea you were expected or I would have made better preparations for you," Cristina said. "When did you come in?"

"Forgive me, but it was very late last night," Roland replied. "One of the footmen let me in and roused the housekeeper to settle me into a room. Outside of that, I was

115

pleased to find my arrival did not wake anyone—unless, perhaps it did."

He gave a quick glance toward Amelie at that statement, but Cristina interrupted with a happy ah-ha.

"So that was the noise in the night! You see, Aunt Tabitha, it was not a ghost, merely Mr. Bentley."

"Was Aunt Tabitha being pestered by spirits again?" Lord Larry asked, filling his plate at the buffet table. "I should have expected that to be more of a problem for Mr. Maitland."

The older man apparently missed the teasing implication of Lord Larry's words. "No sir, I've had no trouble with ghosts at all during my stay here. But if Mrs. Dibbley is certain they are present, I will believe her."

"So you should, sir," the woman insisted. "The spirits *were* restless last night. I'm not a ninny who can't tell the difference between a man shambling around and a ghost."

"Well, I apologize if my shambling woke you," Mr. Bentley said, then added. "Or anyone."

Aunt Tabitha merely sniffed. "You were obviously attempting to be quiet. The ghost was not."

"So we have unquiet spirits in this household, do we?" Lord Larry said, taking his seat at the table. "I hope they don't have nefarious plans for us all."

His wife chastised him gently. "Do stop teasing about it. You don't want to terrorize our guests, do you?"

Lord Larry gave his audience a dark, menacing scowl. "I thought it was up to the ghosts to do that, my love."

"Well, let us hope they do not," Cristina replied, then turned her focus on Mr. Bentley.

"I'm sorry to greet you with such inhospitable banter, Mr. Bentley. Please make yourself welcome. Have you met everyone here?"

"Most everyone," he replied, greeting Lord and Lady

116

Gladbourne, then bowing just slightly toward Amelie. "Miss D'Arnaud, good morning to you."

Drat, but her face was burning again. Was everyone staring at her? She didn't dare look at any of them. Of course Cristina was aware of the history between Amelie and Mr. Bentley; very likely Lady Gladbourne was, too. They must know her discomfort and would clearly wonder how she would react. She could practically feel everyone's eyes on her, awaiting her response.

"It's good to see you again, sir," she managed to utter and hoped it didn't give away anything that she was feeling.

Mr. Bentley seemed to feel none of the awkwardness and torment that she did. In fact, he seemed little more than amused. He replied with a smile that was far too familiar for Amelie's comfort.

"I'm glad to hear it. I was worried that you'd already seen enough of me."

Oh, the horrid man! How could he say something like that? Didn't he realize what images it would evoke in her mind? And what were the others to think as she stammered and blushed in his presence? They might draw conclusions or ask too many questions.

Fortunately, any questions the others might have were set aside. The conversation was neatly interrupted. In fact, Amelie couldn't have asked for a more effective distraction.

Aunt Tabitha shrieked, tossed her teacup across the room, and then fainted dead away.

Chapter 4

"She's coming around! Give her some air."

The ladies bustled around Aunt Tabitha, fussing over her with salts and fans and droplets of water. Mr. Maitland rushed to right the lady's chair, and the other gentlemen were appropriately eager to help. Roland was happy to stand back and let them tend to the matter. He even stood out of the way as one of the servants hurried to pick up the shards of the tea cup from the floor near the buffet table.

"No! Don't touch it!" Aunt Tabitha cried out, rising from where she'd fallen to wave feverishly toward the servant. "It's a dark omen; beware of it, please!"

"Beware of the tea cup?" Lady Gladbourne questioned.

"The tea leaves," Aunt Tabitha said, letting the ladies help her back into her chair. "I'm sorry for all the trouble, but... oh, when I saw what the leaves said, I was overcome."

"The tea leaves said something?" Amelie asked.

"They did! Oh, it's too awful."

As far as Roland knew, tea leaves were not actually capable of speech, but if Larry's Aunt Tabitha seemed to believe that they said something, Roland supposed he could well understand why the shock of it had thrown everyone into a tizzy.

"What, exactly, did your tea leaves say to you?" he asked with honest curiosity.

"A warning. A dark, dire warning."

"How on earth could leaves do that?"

"Young man, I read the leaves. It is an art."

No one outwardly disputed this, and in fact one lady in the group actively nodded in agreement. Roland had not been introduced to her yet, but she did not let that stop her from enthusiastically explaining the older woman's words to him.

"Tea leaves can tell our fortune! I went to a gypsy once who read my leaves for me. Oh, it was fascinating."

Aunt Tabitha nodded approval. "Of course it was. What did they say for you, dear?"

The young woman smiled brightly. "They promised true love! I'm to meet a tall, dark, handsome stranger."

Immediately her gaze shifted to Roland and she batted her eyes. He found himself inclined to stoop and make himself somehow less tall. Pity there was little he could do about the dark and handsome bits.

"The leaves never lie," Aunt Tabitha said, shaking her head.

"But you said your leaves gave a dark omen!" Amelie pointed out.

"It's true, though I wish it were not."

"What sort of omen is it? Do you think something bad is likely to happen?" Mrs. Garville asked.

"It could; it very much could. The leaves warn that... oh, I hate to even speak it."

"Come now, surely you must," Roland encouraged, nearly as desperate to hear what she might say as the worried women huddled around her.

Finally she sighed, pulling herself up straight in her chair and delivering her pronouncement like a statesman. "The leaves warn us that lies and deception are all around. If the truth does not make itself known, before midnight of this day, true love will be doomed."

Oh good God. *That* was the grand decree of the mystic tea leaves? The ladies all seemed quite affected by it, but Roland had to force himself not to laugh. As if the course of true love could be set by some tea leaves! By Jove, this was the demmed strangest house party he'd ever been to.

Lord Gladbourne clearly agreed. "Bits of leaves in the bottom of a cup told you all that?"

Aunt Tabitha was fully returned to her faculties now and eagerly scolded him. "Don't mock the leaves, sir! They say what they say, whether we like it or not. The spirits direct them and now the spirits have spoken."

"And the spirits are concerned about true love," Lord Larry said with just the hint of a sneer. "Well, I suppose I'd rather have that sort of spirit haunting my house than some devilish fiend."

His aunt sneered right back at him. "Take care what you say, Laurence. You might find that you have both."

"Then I defy them to show themselves to me," Lord Larry continued, popping a piece of fruit into his mouth and promptly choking on it.

Lord Gladbourne slapped him on the back and all was well. The ashen look on Larry's wife's face was quite telling, though. She obviously wasn't ready to discount Aunt Tabitha's warning. It seemed to Roland that, as far as the ladies were concerned, ghosts were real and they communicated through tea.

Dash it all if Roland could find any actual proof to discount this.

"I say we let the men go off on their outing," Lady Cristina said finally. "Aunt Tabitha, why don't we retire to the drawing room. I'll have fresh tea brought in and we can sit by the fire. It's gone remarkably chilly today."

Indeed it had. Whether it was the fact that the sun had gone behind clouds and gray light was spilling in through the windows, or that this talk of ghosts and malicious spirits hung over them like a specter, Roland couldn't be sure. All he knew was that, once again, he felt as if things in this house were not as they should be.

He stole a glance at Amelie. She looked away quickly,

unwilling to meet his eyes. He wished he could credit that to some feeling on her part, but at this point, he could not. She'd given no indication that he wasn't the biggest fool imaginable, coming here to this party with the secret hope she might still harbor affection for him.

Between her cool reception and the dreary outlook of the tea leaves, he might do well to abandon all hope now. Of course he wouldn't, though. Cliffside Manor may be full of ghosts, but that was nothing compared to the memories and emotion that haunted Roland every day he had spent without Amelie.

*   *   *

The rest of the morning had been uneventful. Aunt Tabitha had calmed, and eventually decided to retreat to her room for a rest. Poppy Fairwell declared she had letters to write and excused herself to her room, making Amelie want to almost cheer. She had not liked it one bit the way Poppy flitted and flirted for Roland. He seemed to have quite appreciated it, though, making no attempt to ignore her despite the fact that they had not been properly introduced.

Of course they had finally been introduced, probably at Roland's request. Before the ladies took their leave of the men, Lord Larry had made certain to introduce Miss Fairwell. Roland had been quite the gallant about it, too, fawning over her far more than was needed. It was almost as if he were trying to see if he could make Amelie jealous!

Well, she was not some simpering little miss. She could hide her feelings from him just as well as any trained actor. She hardly paid him notice, chatting with Lord Larry, wishing him well on his shoot and laughing at every little thing he said as if she had not a care in the world. At least, she hoped it appeared that way to Roland. It would kill her to think he had any sort of clue how she still felt for him.

Now if only she could be certain her lady friends were equally clueless. They weren't, of course. As she passed the late hours of the morning chatting with Netta and Cristina, it became painfully obvious. The time had come to discuss Mr. Bentley.

"I am happy that you do not seem the least bit upset about Mr. Bentley's unexpected arrival," Cristina said bravely.

It was just the three of them in the cozy drawing room. The fire crackled in the grate, a ginger cat had curled up on Amelie's lap, and everything around them spoke comfort and warmth. It was as good a time as any to get the matter out in the open and have done with it. She put down her needle work and smiled for her friends.

"I'm sure you've both been worrying for me, and I thank you, but be assured it's not necessary."

"You are not upset that Mr. Bentley is here?"

"Do I appear to be upset?" she said with monumental calm.

"No, you don't," Cristina said. "And that's what worries me. You were engaged to the man, until he jilted you. Larry was being quite thoughtless to invite him to join us, knowing your history."

"He did not jilt me," Amelie insisted. "He simply did not wish to marry me, so I let him go. It was amicable."

"Still, I hate that it must make you uncomfortable."

"I'm quite fine, really. We are bound to be in company once in a while, so you mustn't worry. He has his interests, and I have mine."

"Yes, I noticed his interest when Larry introduced them," Cristina said. "Miss Fairwell very nearly threw herself at him, didn't she?"

Netta laughed. "As much as she does every man. Honestly, perhaps your husband is safe from her because she's your cousin, but I intend to keep a close watch over

Gladbourne while she is around."

"She's harmless," Cristina assured. "She doesn't want to
steal someone's husband, she wants to snag one of her
own."

They giggled. It was very funny for the other ladies,
indeed, because they had wonderful husbands they could
trust not to look twice at someone like Poppy. They had
love and commitment in their pockets and future happiness
was assured. It wasn't so funny for Amelie. Aside from
Netta's father, Mr. Bentley was the only unattached man at
this house party. Like it or not, he was the one and only
prime target for Poppy.

And he definitely had seemed to like it.

"She'd better not get her hopes too high on Mr.
Bentley," Netta said, eyes flashing.

"Why do you say that?" Cristina asked.

"If she wants a husband she'll end up disappointed.
He'll likely jilt her, too."

Amelie ground her teeth as the other ladies laughed.
She hated that she still felt such loyalty to Roland that she
couldn't even chuckle at his expense. Worse, she hated that
she doubted he would jilt Miss Fairwell. He was not a cruel
man. He had simply been cruel to Amelie.

"I say you are well rid of him," Cristina declared.
"Perhaps this visit is a good thing. Time has healed your
wounds and you will see you are better off now."

"Exactly," Netta agreed. "You can see him with wiser
eyes and realize just what he is."

"A jilt and a bounder and a scoundrel," Cristina added,
just in case Amelie hadn't quite seen him as all of that yet.

"You can do much better than him," Netta said. "This
spring you must visit us in London and I'll make sure
Gladbourne brings around all of his bachelor friends."

"Just think how Mr. Bentley will suffer when you are

happily wed to an earl!" Cristina said gleefully. "He'll rue his mistake, for sure."

She probably would have gone on, joyfully plotting Roland's unhappy future, but a maid interrupted to say that Aunt Tabitha was calling for her. Cristina quickly excused herself and went to see what troubling omen the poor dear was worried over now. Amelie hoped it was nothing too bothersome, but she was glad for the break in conversation.

Try as she might, she just couldn't find it in herself to wish ill for Roland Bentley.

"I hope you don't think we are amusing ourselves at your expense," Netta said when they were alone. "It's just hard for us to feel much fondness for the man who has caused you pain."

"I'm lucky to have such good friends," Amelie assured her. "You give no offense."

"Good. I think Cristina might be a little too harsh on Mr. Bentley as she knows you far better than she does him. It's only natural that she would take your side over his."

"She's welcome to dislike him as much as she pleases. As far as I'm concerned, it's an ancient matter and nothing any of us need to concern ourselves over. Far more current, of course, are the happy unions of both of you. How lucky that things worked out so well. Lord Gladbourne seems quite an excellent gentleman."

Netta smiled and her cheeks blushed bright pink. Amelie had known it was a good idea to redirect the course of their conversation. Bringing up Lord Gladbourne instantly put all thoughts of Roland Bentley out of Netta's head and there was no doubt that subject happily off the table.

"He is very excellent," Netta said, and proceeded to relate a long monotony of her husband's many fine qualities. Apparently, not only was he generous and kind, but he also had very fine feet. Amelie preferred not to think about that.

Instead, she immersed herself in her stitching. The cat kneaded the pillow beside her and purred loudly. Netta droned on, reciting the entertaining story of how she had been supposed to marry Lord Larry, but somehow manipulated her way out of that so that she could win the heart of her beloved Gladbourne. It made for a very relaxing few minutes, especially because no one made any mention of Roland Bentley or questioned Amelie's feelings about him.

Until, sadly, Netta ran out of story and came around, once again, to Amelie's.

"So do you have any interests?" she asked.

"I'm fond of gardening," Amelie answered.

"No, not that sort of interest, the more interesting kind: romance."

"Heavens, you said I have any interest in that?"

"You did! You said Mr. Bentley has his interests and you have yours. So please, tell an old married woman all of the details."

"Oh, well... that is, I—"

Netta fairly squealed at her. "But look at you, Amelie! How you blush. So someone *has* captured your interest. Go on, who is he?"

Drat it all, but of course Amelie did feel her cheeks turning red. Again. Netta had brought up the subject of romance and instantly all Amelie could think of was Roland and how he had appeared when she'd walked in on him last night. Good gracious, but the more she tried to wash that image from her mind, the more she could think of nothing else! And her face was giving all of it away to dear Netta.

"He's no one."

Netta was too smart for that. "Of course he is someone

126

or you wouldn't go all pink and agitated like this. Now come, it's just us. I've told you all sorts of things about my romantic affairs. The least you could do is return the favor."

"Your romantic affair is with your own husband. I hardly have anything like that to discuss."

"You're dying to tell me about him, I just know it."

"No, really I'm not."

"You'd rather keep him a secret? Very well. I'm quite good at guessing. He's someone I know, isn't he?"

"How can you know that?"

"Because if I didn't know him you wouldn't hesitate to tell me about him," Netta said, smiling coyly. "Now, let me guess who he is..."

"No, we will not play this game."

Netta ignored her and continued. "Is he someone Cristina knows?"

"Yes, but—"

"Ah ha! That narrows it."

"I'm not going to tell you. Even if you guess, I'll deny."

Netta chewed her lip and contemplated. "There must be a reason it's such a secret. Hmm, perhaps he is not someone we would approve?"

Amelie clamped her mouth shut and refused to even so much as look at her friend. The game had gone on long enough and she was determined Netta had all the information she was going to get.

Except that even her silence was telling. Netta squealed again.

"Oh! But he *is* someone we wouldn't approve! Good heavens, Amelie. How scandalous of you. Who is this mystery man you're keeping so secret?"

"No one. Oh, look at the time. Surely the men will return from shooting soon and your husband will demand your attention. For myself, I think a nap is in order. Just look at me yawning."

"You are faking to get out of this conversation," Netta accused.

"And it's working," Amelie said, putting the cat off her lap and returning her needlework to the basket behind her chair.

Netta laughed in good fun, shaking her head. "Very well, you win this match. But don't think I'll let you keep this secret forever."

Oh, yes she would keep it forever. As long as her heart still ached for Roland Bentley, no living person would have any clue of it.

Chapter 5

Roland ducked around the corner to avoid being seen. The men had indeed returned from shooting. The others had gone up to their rooms to change clothes, but he'd lingered behind to brood. He'd spent the whole morning fretting over what he'd witnessed just before they had left.

His friend Larry had been overly friendly with Amelie. Clearly they hadn't thought he'd noticed. The ladies were taking their leave from the breakfast room and Roland had just been introduced to Miss Fairwell. She was quite a talker and Larry must have thought she held all of Roland's attention. While Larry's wife tended to the ailing Aunt Tabitha, Larry and Amelie had shared a moment of obvious kinship. Or perhaps more than that.

During the men's outing that followed, Roland listened intently to everything Larry said, searching for any hint that he was playing more than just host to Miss D'Arnaud. The man was cagey, though. When Roland brought up her name, the best he could detect from Larry was a sense of protectiveness. He couldn't be sure, but it might just have bordered on possessiveness.

Connecting that to the fact that the footsteps he'd heard in the night had led from the Garville suite to Amelie's bedroom, it was difficult for Roland not to wonder what was going on there. Was Amelie D'Arnaud on better than friendly terms with the husband of one of her best friends? Roland had not wanted to believe it.

In fact, when he heard Amelie's voice in the drawing room as he wandered past, he'd stopped to listen purely in hope of disproving his theory. If everything was rosey between Amelie and Mrs. Garville, then surely that would signify something. Unfortunately, what he'd heard had done the opposite of that. Damn it, but his worst fears were apparently true.

Mrs. Garville was not even in company with Amelie just now. Amelie was with Lady Gladbourne, who was raving about her magnificent husband. It was enough to turn Roland's stomach, really, but then she'd shifted the conversation onto Amelie. Did Miss D'Arnaud have any romantic interest? Of course there was no way Roland could have walked away before hearing the answer to that.

He wished he had, though. The last thing he'd wanted to hear was the truth. Amelie had found a new love, and it was Lord Larry.

She'd admitted it to Lady Gladbourne. No, she hadn't used Larry's name specifically, but Lady Gladbourne had needled her for details. Everything Amelie said fit Larry perfectly: he was someone who must be kept secret, he was someone the other ladies knew, and he was certainly someone they would not approve.

The fury and pain that boiled inside Roland nearly knocked him over. He'd lost her for good, hadn't he? He knew what this meant. She was a decent woman; there was no way she would undertake an affair with a married man if she didn't truly love him. Amelie must honestly love Lord Larry, and that meant she did not—and never would—love Roland.

That didn't take away from the fact that Larry was married and what they were doing was wrong. Terribly wrong! Roland couldn't stand by and let it continue.

Damn it, he wouldn't. As long as he was here in this house, decency behooved him to make things as hard as possible for those two tainted lovebirds. Lord Larry worried about ghosts? Well, he was just about to find out what it was to be truly haunted.

*   *   *

Dinner was a slightly quieter affair than breakfast. Granted, there were no episodes of Aunt Tabitha breaking dishes and swooning away, but conversation felt just a bit stifled. Amelie really couldn't guess why, but she was happy that Netta had not tormented her by reintroducing the matter of their earlier discussion.

It was hard enough to merely sit across the table from Roland Bentley, let alone be reminded that her feelings for him were nearly so transparent that Netta could guess them. She prayed no one watched her very closely tonight. Mr. Bentley seemed to be doing enough of that for everyone and it had created the most extraordinary butterflies in her insides.

"So I take it shooting today was somewhat successful," Cristina asked over a forkful of pheasant.

"Especially so for your own husband," Lord Gladbourne replied. "He can be thanked for the great bounty of our meal today."

"I'll claim the advantage of being in my own field," Lord Larry replied, then added. "Although generally Roland is a far superior shot than I am. I do wonder what has the man all distracted today?"

"Perhaps it is all the talk of ghosts," Lady Gladbourne suggested and Amelie could have hugged her for not laying suspicion at her own feet.

"I think we've not had enough talk of ghosts," Aunt Tabitha piped up. "We are growing closer to the end of the day and I cannot help but wonder what they have in store for us this night."

"Perhaps extra vigilance is called for," Roland said, surprisingly without facetious eye-roll or any sign that he mocked the older woman.

"What's this?" Lord Larry said. "You're now a believer

131

in all of the wild stories?"

"I simply suggest we approach the matter with logic. If strange things are happening unseen, perhaps the best thing to do is to watch more attentively," Roland replied.

Cristina cocked her head and considered his suggestion. "You are saying we make a concerted effort to uncover the source of Aunt Tabitha's worries?"

Poppy seemed to suddenly comprehend the theme of this discourse and she cried out in glee. "A ghost hunt! You are suggesting a ghost hunt tonight. Oh, Mr. Bentley, what a splendid idea."

The others latched onto this with remarkable interest. Amelie, of course, was not nearly so eager to go prowling through the dark manor, searching for the very thing that had terrified her nearly to death. She could hardly use her own experience as proof to dissuade them, though. What was she to do?

"I think it's a capital idea," Lord Larry said as the group's enthusiasm grew. "We could break into teams and spread out, searching the house thoroughly. I will select my lovely wife for my team, of course."

"I want to be on Mr. Bentley's team," Poppy said quickly. "It was his idea, after all."

It was fairly obvious how the teams would select themselves, each couple pairing off and Mr. Maitland vowing to stay guard over Aunt Tabitha. Simple mathematics let Amelie know instantly that she would be left alone. Apparently Cristina could make sums, too.

"But we are an uneven number," she said, frowning. "We cannot leave one person alone."

"Then Miss D'Arnaud should accompany us, my dearest," Lord Larry said. "We would welcome her company."

"But that leaves Miss Fairwell unchaperoned with a

132

gentleman," Aunt Tabitha said. "I cannot allow that. Indeed, if we are to do this thing, we should all go in groups of three."

"A wise proposition," Mr. Maitland said. "I will accompany my daughter and her husband, and if you are inclined, then you should go with Mr. Bentley and Miss Fairwell."

"Are you sure you are up for this, Aunt Tabitha?" Cristina asked. "We do not wish to overtax you."

"I was born for this, my dear," the older woman assured her, light glinting in her eye. "No doubt it is exactly what is needed for this situation."

"Very well," Lord Larry said, pushing back from the table and indicating that the servants could clear this last course. "Let us retire to the drawing room and make our plans for the night. We'll need lamps, and I'll draw out a rough design of the manor so everyone can find their way."

"It's quite a labyrinth, I'll tell you," Cristina said. "We don't even use a good portion of the house as it's awaiting repairs."

The dark, ominous feel of anticipation began to creep up Amelie's spine. This whole thing was spiraling rapidly. She'd had no time to convince the group it was a bad idea, and now she'd been sucked in. Lord Larry was making plans for her and even Aunt Tabitha seemed to conclude this was just the thing for them.

A quick glance at Roland as they all rose to leave the room and her spirits sank even lower. Roland glared disapproval at her, as if he knew she ought to decry this, but did not. Indeed, he must wonder why she could have been so convinced of ghosts one day and willing to participate in this folly the next. She couldn't quite understand it herself.

"One thing we all need to remember," Aunt Tabitha said, pausing to halt the movement of the group at the doorway. "By midnight tonight, the truth must be revealed. Whatever that means, we should all be prepared."

The ladies exchanged worried glances—except for Poppy, who seemed oblivious to Aunt Tabitha's dire tone— but the men gave no indication they were at all intimidated. Lord Larry, especially. He grinned and offered one arm to his wife and one arm to Amelie.

"I, for one, am prepared for quite a lark," he said cheerfully. "After all, what's the worst that could happen?"

Amelie shuddered at his words. She knew the answer to his question all too well. What was the worst that could happen on a ghost hunt? That they would find one, of course.

Chapter 6

Roland led the way down a long, narrow passage. Miss Fairwell clung to his arm and Aunt Tabitha trailed behind, muttering under her breath. How had he gotten dragged into this? Worse, everyone seemed to think it was his idea.

Well, it was not. His idea would have been to stalk Larry and catch him in the act of behaving badly with Amelie. To put an end to any entanglement there would certainly be far more satisfying for Roland than locating some mythical disembodied phantom.

For now, however, he was hunting ghosts. This part of the house was old, dusty, and if it wasn't infested with ghosts it certainly did have plenty of corporeal inhabitants. Mice scurried in the corners, spiders spun webs across the walkways, and occasionally something fluttered and screeched overhead.

Miss Fairwell used all of this to illicit constant reassurance and attention from Roland. He was growing more than a little weary of it. If not for the fact that he'd have to live with himself afterward, he had half a mind to dump both trembling women in an anteroom and stalk off to find Amelie.

There was no telling what she was up to with Lord Larry right now. *Demme* the man for his faithlessness! He had a perfectly good wife of his own. Why did he need to take up with Amelie, too?

"This corridor ends in a stairway," Miss Fairwell noted, as if Roland didn't have eyes of his own. "Should we go up, or should we go down?"

Roland was about to reply when a loud, sharp rap echoed around them. It was as if someone were pounding a walking stick against the floor directly above them. Miss Fairwell jumped and dug her fingernails into Roland's coat. The lamplight flickered over the walls and the ceiling as Aunt Tabitha waved it around.

"We are not alone," she said in a low, creaking voice.

"It could be a mouse," Roland suggested.

"A giant, evil mouse!" Miss Fairwell whimpered.

"Who was assigned to hunt on the floor above us?" Roland asked.

It took Miss Fairwell a moment to realize she was the one holding the paper for their group. A plan had been laid out and assignments given. Roland took the page from her trembling hand and studied it. From what he could see, no one had been assigned to the floor above them. The other teams were in more distant wings of the house. According to what had been agreed to, this team should be alone in this wing. There was no one here to be rapping that floor.

"I say we should go down the stairs," Miss Fairwell suggested. "Not up."

"I think you are right," Aunt Tabitha concurred. "Here, Mr. Bentley, carry the lamp. You should go first."

Of course he should. If a malicious spirit from the depths of hell were to leap out and accost them, as a gentleman, he should die first. But he took the lamp and moved toward the staircase. He had to admit, down did seem to be the best option just now.

The dank air came alive with the glow of their lamp, the odd angles of this twisting staircase creating tortured shadows and unnatural shapes all around them. Miss Fairwell was practically plastered to his back so he moved slowly, carefully, peering into the darkness around each turn. The decrepit wood of the stair treads creaked and groaned with every step that they took.

Whose blasted idea was this ghost hunt, anyway?

136

Roland was determined to have words with them once this was over. If he survived it, which he began to doubt when a tread gave way and his foot crashed through the rotted wood.

Miss Fairwell shrieked, but he righted himself and held her from falling. The lamp swung wildly around, making it nearly impossible to see clearly. One of the ever-present spiders dropped down into his collar. Dash it all, but this was *not* the way he had pictured his first evening at the house party where he had come with specific hopes of winning back the love of his life.

"Here, step close to the center column of the staircase," he advised, leading the ladies around the broken tread. "We have reached the bottom, so you will be steady here."

The stairway opened into what appeared to be a workroom, of sorts. Clearly this part of the manor was originally intended for servant use, although no one but the vermin seemed to have any use for it right now. Roland stepped inside, holding the lamp high for maximum light to allow the ladies safe entrance.

Miss Fairwell hopped off the last tread of the stairway, brushing cobwebs from her hair and shuddering with horror at, apparently, everything. Roland waited for Aunt Tabitha, but she did not appear. He'd not heard her stumble on that damned broken stair, but perhaps she had. He rushed back to the staircase with the lamp.

"Here is the light," he called around the turn. "Can you see to find your way?"

The woman did not answer. Cold dread gripped him. She must have fallen and he'd left her behind! He ran up the twisting steps, two at a time.

The broken one nearly tripped him again, but he made it all the way to the top without finding Aunt Tabitha or her pitiful corpse. Where the devil could she have gone?

"Mr. Bentley!" Miss Fairwell called from below. "Don't

leave me here! It's dark and there are... things running over my feet!"

Hellfire. He couldn't take the lamp to hunt for Aunt Tabitha and leave Miss Fairwell behind. He might want to, but he couldn't. Cursing under his breath, he marched back down the stairs, missing that broken tread this time, but nearly falling through another.

"I can see why this part of the house is unused," he grumbled.

"Where is Mrs. Dibbley?" Miss Fairwell asked nervously.

"I couldn't find her," he said.

"Do you think something got her?"

"No, I think the dotty old bird went off on her own."

"Why would she do that? Oh, but this is dreadful. What will happen to her, Mr. Bentley?"

"She'll likely fall through a rotted stairway, I should think."

"That's awful. She should go after her."

"Where? I went up to the top and didn't see any sign of her. She could be anywhere by now. She used to live here, if you recall. I daresay she knows her way through these rooms far better than we do."

"But why would she go off on her own? Who knows what dangerous things roam about here."

Roland had a growing suspicion that Aunt Tabitha knew exactly how many dangerous things roamed about here and that the answer was zero. The house itself was a menace, but they'd still seen no sign of a ghost. If that old woman was willing to go off on her own, it could only mean she knew there was no danger. She claimed something haunted these corridors? Roland was beginning to think Aunt Tabitha knew much more about that than she professed.

"Oh look!" Miss Fairwell cried, pointing toward the end of the long corridor that led off of the work room. "I believe I see a light."

And so she did. Roland noticed just dim flashes at first, but there was definitely some sort of light in that direction. And it seemed to be getting brighter.

"Perhaps we have found Aunt Tabitha," he said, leading a still shaking Miss Fairwell toward it.

It turned out not to be Aunt Tabitha. They came to the end of the corridor and followed the light around a corner, into an old medieval hall. A huge hearth dominated the center of the room, and all manner of stuffed beasts hung along the wall, surrounded by rusted, dusty weapons and armor. The light they had followed was a lamp exactly like theirs, held by a slightly bored looking Lord Gladbourne.

Mr. Maitland's voice carried over the room as he recited at length the various coats of arms prominently displayed behind what must have, at one time, been a banquet table. The ladies cried out happy greetings as the two groups converged.

"I was beginning to think we were the only people left in this whole house," Lady Gladbourne said.

"So you've seen nothing of anyone else?" Miss Fairwell asked.

"We've seen spiders and mice, and all these lovely creatures," Lord Gladbourne answered, sweeping his arm wide to display the boars and deer and even a bear's head glaring down from their plaques on the wall. "But you are the first humans, living or dead."

"This is the great hall," Mr. Maitland announced. "This house has been in the Garville family since before Cromwell."

"But where is Aunt Tabitha?" Lady Gladbourne asked.

"Wasn't she with you?" Mr. Maitland asked, taking his focus off the ancient collection and scanning the room for his friend.

"She was, but she's missing," Roland explained.

"We came down a staircase, and by the time we were at the bottom, she was gone!" Miss Fairwell said. "Mr. Bentley searched for her, but we don't know where she's gone."

Clearly this was more than enough to concern the other group, as well. Mr. Maitland especially.

"We have to find her," he said. "Where could she be?"

"We heard some noise in an upper level, and then she was just gone," Miss Fairwell said.

Mr. Maitland was ready for action. "Well, we must start a search! Where is this staircase?"

"I don't advise it," Roland said. "It was a servant access, and already two of the treads have crumbled away. I can't say that it would even support another attempt."

"But there is another staircase just over this way," Lady Gladbourne said, indicating a wide doorway at the other side of the hall. "If Aunt Tabitha is upstairs on the next level, then we could go that way."

"What if she is not on that level?" Mr. Maitland said quickly. "She could be lost and alone following behind you. If we all go upstairs, who will be here for her?"

"You're suggesting we should split up again?" Lord Gladbourne asked.

"Yes," Mr. Maitland answered. "I will go upstairs and hunt there while the rest of you hunt on this level."

"Papa, you should not have to go alone," Lady Gladbourne said.

"I insist, my pet. And see? Here is an old sconce lamp. This will give all the light I will need."

He had pulled an old lantern off the wall and was already helping himself to a light from the lamp Lord Gladbourne carried. The rickety lantern sputtered aglow.

"See? I will find my way."

"But we should remain a team, Papa, and—"

"Wait, did you hear that noise?" Mr. Maitland said suddenly.

Roland hadn't heard anything, but Miss Fairwell jumped and insisted that she'd heard it, too. Lord and Lady Gladbourned just looked confused.

"Find Tabitha!" Mr. Maitland said. "She could be in danger."

Before any of them could argue, he hurried from the room, the flickering glow from his lamp spilling a feeble pool before him as he left the great hall in the direction of that staircase they had mentioned.

"Well," Lord Gladbourne said after a moment of stunned silence. "Do we follow him?"

"I don't like to think of him going off all alone," Lady Gladbourne replied. "Maybe we should—"

She was cut off by the perfect response. A sound pierced the night, shrill and insistent. In a house full of ghosts, disappearing guests, and crumbling staircases, Roland felt it was the cap to an already eventful evening.

Somewhere in the distant depths of the dark, sprawling manor, a woman screamed. Roland knew in his soul who it was: *Amelie!*

Chapter 7

Amelie trailed behind Cristina and Lord Larry as they followed the warm glow of their lamplight through desolate corridors and forgotten rooms. When Cristina said the house was a labyrinth, she hadn't been exaggerating. Cliffside Manor sprawled on and on, a mash of architectural styles and various eras of additions. The fact that the hour was getting late and wisps of clouds obscured the moonlight that attempted to filter through the dim windows only added to the fearsome feel of the place.

They'd been wandering aimlessly since their ghost hunt had begun. Lord Larry carried the map he'd drawn up for them but it seemed he wasn't bothering to use it. Amelie assumed this was simply because he knew his own home better than his new wife and a guest, but when they found themselves in a room she knew for a fact they had passed through before, she wasn't so certain. Did Lord Larry have a clue where he was taking them, or were they hopelessly lost?

"We've been here before," Cristina mentioned.

"Er, yes," Larry conceded. "This room has doorways leading to rooms that give access to other more distant areas of the house. We've made a complete circuit."

"I don't think we've gone this way," Cristina suggested, peeking into the darkness through one of the several doorways.

"Yes, I'm sure that we have," her husband said. "Let's go this way instead."

"No, that's the doorway we went through last time," Cristina replied.

"I don't believe so, my dearest. You must have gotten

turned around."

Amelie had to speak up. "No, I'm quite sure Cristina is right about this one. We haven't gone through this doorway yet. Where does it lead?"

"Nowhere," Lord Larry said quickly. "A servant's access, that's all."

But Cristina was still peering. "It's a corridor, and I think I see light at the end of it."

"Probably just a window with moonlight coming through," Lord Larry said.

Amelie couldn't help but wonder why the man was so determined to dissuade them from going this way. She moved to Cristina's side and looked into the black corridor. Just as her friend had said, a dim light could barely be seen there.

"The moon is behind clouds tonight," Cristina said. "No, this light is from a candle, I think. Come, we should go this way."

Without waiting for her husband, she stepped through the doorway. Amelie had a moment of hesitation, but decided to follow. Lord Larry could do nothing but hurry behind them, bringing the lamp to light up their way.

"It's just an old access, to allow servants to and from the kitchens," he said.

"Well, we should investigate," Cristina insisted. "If I were a ghost, this is most certainly the type of dark, lonely place I would haunt."

"Let's all be thankful you aren't a ghost," Amelie said with a shudder.

"Look, what was that?" Cristina said suddenly, halting in her tracks.

"It was nothing," Lord Larry said. "Are you ready to turn back now?"

Apparently Cristina was not. She crept forward, slowly.

"The light up ahead, it flickered."

"I saw it, too," Amelie admitted. "It flickered and dimmed, as if something passed in front of it."

"Well, if it was something solid to block light, then it couldn't have been a ghost," Lord Larry reasoned. "We should go back and try another route."

"Absolutely not," his wife persisted. "Laurence Garville, are you afraid?"

"Afraid of my own home? No, I am not. I am simply trying to make your ghost hunt an interesting one, and for that I think we should leave off being distracted by shadows and go find a ghost."

Cristina merely laughed at that and muttered under her breath. It sounded vaguely Spanish, which made sense considering Cristina's father was a nobleman from that country. She seemed to have inherited his bold Latin nature.

"I think whatever we'll find up ahead will be more than interesting enough," she assured her husband, pressing on.

They had come far enough along the narrow corridor that Amelie could see the source of the light. It did indeed glow and flicker like a candle and it spilled out of a room. Who on earth would have come all the way back here to light a candle? At least she could take comfort that it was not a ghost. In her experience, they needed no candles to facilitate their ghoulish prowling.

"What do you suppose is inside?" Cristina asked as they approached.

"We could still turn back," Lord Larry suggested.

"Not on your life!" Cristina said, hurrying the last few steps to the doorway.

She disappeared, turning the corner and entering the room. Amelie rushed to catch up to her. Whatever horrors might be within, she refused to allow her friend to face them alone. Stalwart Lord Larry took his sweet time tagging along.

The room they entered was small, and made smaller by the great quantities of fabric draped over everything. Brocades and silks covered furniture, cascaded over the walls, and puddled on the floor. Pillows were scattered here and there. It was as if they had walked into a Moroccan pavilion.

As Amelie looked closer, though, she amended this thought. It was less like a harem room and more like a gypsy caravan. A low table sat in the center of the room and on it were several implements. The most obvious item was a crystal ball. Next to it, the waxy stub of a candle glowed and sputtered. The elegant holder for this candle was a dirty old skull, greeting them with its wide, mocking smile.

"Good heavens, look at that!" Cristina gasped.

"What is this place?" Amelie asked, moving timidly to examine the things on the table.

"I would guess someone has been using this room in an effort to contact the spirits," Lord Larry offered.

"Or foresee the future," Amelie added.

She crouched down over the table. Spread out on before her was an unlikely assortment of small objects; bits of bone, jagged potsherds of clay, and smooth round stones. All of the items, she noted, had strange symbols carved into or painted on them. She was hesitant to touch any of them.

"What is this?" she wondered aloud.

"Gypsy runes," Cristina replied. "I've seen them before."

"You've seen them?" Lord Larry questioned.

Now Cristina seemed just slightly embarrassed. "Yes, in the past. My father's family in Spain... well, there is some Rom in my bloodline. I had a great grandmother who came from gypsy people."

"I had no idea," Lord Larry said.

"And my very proper mother would be mortified if she knew I had told you!" Cristina insisted. "Please, you mustn't mention it. That part of my ancestry is not well publicized, as you can imagine."

"You are a perfect English Rose as far as I'm concerned," he said, smiling lovingly at her.

Cristina smiled back and Amelie was fairly certain she heard a wistful sigh escape her friend as the couple made cow's eyes and exchanged meaningful looks. Amelie cleared her throat.

"So what do these gypsy runes mean?" she asked.

Cristina brought her attention back to them, leaning in for a good look. "It's been so long... but I think I recall some of these signs. This one is... Oh, yes I see what it says."

"Well?" Amelie prodded.

"They warn of deception... and death."

This odd coincidence was not lost on Amelie. "The same thing Aunt Tabitha saw in her tea leaves."

The candle flickered. The room was suddenly cold. Was Amelie imagining, or did the grin on that foul skull spread even wider, baring its teeth in defiance or warning? Anxious chills ran over her arms and the hair at her neck prickled alert.

"I think we should go now," Cristina said, backing away from the table.

"Yes, we should... wait, what is this?" Amelie said, her eye catching on something at the edge of the table, just beyond the grinning skull.

She reached, clutching a small glittery object in her hand.

"What is it?" Cristina asked.

"Aunt Tabitha's brooch. The one she is never without."

Suddenly the candle went out. A wind breezed through

the room, dousing the flame and the lamp in Lord Larry's hand, as well. They were in sudden darkness.

Worse than that, they were not alone. Hands reached out of the darkness, grabbing at Amelie, fumbling at her as if to tear even breath from her. She screamed, clambering to her feet and staggering to the doorway. She found the door frame and felt her way out into the corridor.

Nothing mattered but escape now. The darkness closed around her and she knew only one thing: she must flee for her very life.

Chapter 8

Roland had directed his group to split up. Lord and Lady Gladbourne went off in one direction, and Roland took Miss Fairwell with him in another. She was rather a nervous wreck now as they searched the house not for some mythical ghost, but an actual person in obvious distress. It was clear this was no longer a simple game meant for mere entertainment.

Damn it all, but Amelie's life was at stake! Roland simply had to find her.

"I need to rest," Miss Fairwell complained. "We must have covered every room in this house by now."

"Obviously not, or we would have discovered Miss D'Arnaud."

"How can you be sure that was her? Maybe it was Aunt Tabitha."

"It was *her*." And, by God, he was going to find her.

"I didn't realize you knew her so very well."

"Well enough." *Not hardly, but enough to know that had been her scream.*

"She must be fine now," Miss Fairwell said, pausing to lean against the polished wood paneling in the empty room they had just searched. "We've not heard any more screams for the longest time."

It was true; they'd not heard anything for quite some time now. Roland couldn't imagine that was a good thing. He prayed that scream from Amelie hadn't been her last breath on this earth.

Where could she be? He went to the tall, multi-paned window in their room and stared out. The moon was still obscured by clouds, giving little light to aid in their search.

The house was huge, dark and foreboding. For all his efforts so far, he was no closer to finding Amelie than he had been when they started.

Where could she be? He crossed to the small anteroom that led off to the side. It was as empty as it had been the first time he'd checked it and there was no other way into or out of it.

Nothing. This hunt was revealing nothing and he was running out of places to look. That blasted map Lord Larry had drawn was woefully incomplete. Still, it couldn't hurt to take yet another look at it.

He called for Miss Fairwell. "Bring me the map again."

She obviously did not understand the gravity of the situation because she didn't even have the good grace to reply. Frustrated, he left the anteroom and went back to the main room where he'd left her. He needed that map to give him some direction, more places to search.

But the map—and Miss Fairwell—was gone! Hellfire, the girl had just vanished. One moment she'd been there, the next moment she was gone. How could this happen?

Roland glared over every inch of the room. There was no furniture, no nook, nowhere for her to hide. The only doorway into the room was at the far end, and the floorboards creaked so loudly he would have heard if she'd gone that way. Just to be sure, he rushed out there and waved the lamp up and down.

No sign of her. He called, of course, but there was no answer. Miss Fairwell had vanished, just as Aunt Tabitha had. Perhaps the same thing had happened to Amelie, only she'd had the chance to cry out. What in God's name was this? Who was absconding with their women?

And what was happening to them once they were gone?

The possibilities were too terrifying to imagine. Roland needed to get a hold of himself and go find the others. He rushed out to the corridor and tried to remember which direction to go. It wasn't a difficult decision; the sound of footsteps approaching grabbed his attention.

But they weren't just footsteps, they were rapid footsteps. Someone was running toward him up the corridor. Not sure if this would be friend or foe, he hid his lamp around the doorframe and ducked back into the room. The footsteps were getting louder.

Any minute now, he'd intercept whoever this was. Perhaps he'd finally get some answers.

*   *   *

Amelie could still feel the hands in the dark, clawing at her. Her chest ached from running, but she didn't dare slow down. Without a lamp, she'd been fumbling in the dark, knocking about carelessly in a mad effort to get away from whatever had attacked her in that mystical room. Her conscience pricked horribly, too. In her terror she'd left Cristina and Lord Larry behind.

Perhaps there was hope ahead of her, though. She'd felt her way to another corridor and had begun following it. Far ahead of her now she could barely see the faint glow of light. It was dim, almost hidden from view, but she'd seen it and she was aiming for it.

Her heart pounded as her footsteps sped up. She prayed she would find help when she reached that light, and not further terror. Somewhere there had to be someone who could help her, could return with her to locate poor Cristina and her husband. With any luck she'd not be too late.

The light had gone even dimmer now, yet she was sure she was getting closer. She increased her pace, determined to find whoever had been there to light up the way. Perhaps if she called out, she could catch his attention—

She didn't get the chance, though. Once again, hands reached out and clutched her. She struggled, kicking furiously and flailing her arms. Someone massive and strong had darted out of a doorway and was holding her tightly. She had to escape.

"Amelie, it's me!"

Roland! His voice was soft and low in her ear. The most beautiful sound she could imagine, but she wasn't imagining. He was real!

She let her terrified, exhausted body go limp. Thank heavens, she had found him. He wrapped his arms around her and she buried her face in his wonderful warmth.

"I've got you," he assured her. "You're safe with me."

But of course she wasn't safe. She had to force herself to let go, to think of someone else finally. The danger was real and her friends back there needed her.

"You have to help them," she said, struggling to catch her breath.

"Who? What happened?"

"We found a room with a skull and strange objects... and someone was after us! Please, you have to come help."

"Of course, but who am I helping?"

"Lord Larry, of course."

He was suddenly not quite as warm. "Lord Larry?"

"And Cristina. Someone came out of the dark and grabbed me. I screamed and ran away, but I don't know what happened to them."

"You left Lord Larry behind?"

As if she didn't already feel guilty enough about that. How dare he make her feel worse. She pushed him away and glared up at him.

"I was terrified for my life and wasn't thinking clearly. I ran, yes, but now we can go back there and help them."

"You left Larry behind."

"I already admitted it, and I feel dreadful," she said. "Poor Cristina must be petrified. Will you come help me

152

now?"

"Of course," he said, ignoring her protests and putting his arms around her again. "Catch your breath, and we'll be off."

Catch her breath? How on earth could she do that in his embrace? He was so gentle with her, so careful, she could hardly think straight, let alone breathe. So many years she'd dreamed of this, of being back in his arms and hearing his voice. She couldn't even think about catching her breath.

"Which way do we go?" he asked after a moment.

She shoved all the warm, dreamy thoughts aside and forced herself back to the present. Cristina and Lord Larry needed them. She had to concentrate on that, no matter how much she'd rather curl up in Roland's arms and forget everything else.

"I'm not really sure," she said honestly. "I was running in the dark, tripping into corners and feeling my way."

He considered a moment, keeping one arm around her but taking up a lamp with the other and peering into the corridor. "Well, you were coming from that direction, so I would guess that is the way we should go."

"Yes, that sounds right," she agreed.

Her heart was pounding less furiously now and her head was beginning to clear. Roland still stayed close to her, but they were walking confidently along the corridor that, apparently, she'd just run through. If not for the prickling fear and the threat of bodily harm, spending the night alone with Roland in this forsaken wing might be quite lovely.

But wait, how could she be alone with him? They'd broken into teams. Where were his teammates?

"Shouldn't we wait for the others?" she asked, pausing to look over her shoulder.

"What others?" he asked.

"Aunt Tabitha and Miss Fairwell."

"Oh. Them. Well, Aunt Tabitha disappeared coming down a staircase, and Miss Fairwell disappeared back there in that room."

"Disappeared? Good heavens, what do you mean?"

"I mean one minute they were there, the next they were not. It's the damnedest thing, I tell you."

She was stunned by this news, and more grateful than ever for Roland's sturdy arm to cling to and the light from his glowing lamp. What could have happened to his partners? For half of a second she wondered if she could trust his telling of the story, but of course she would trust him. This was Roland, after all. He might break off an engagement and tear her heart in two, but he would never cause actual harm to anyone else.

And she had to admit, it was rather handy to be rid of Miss Fairwell. The chit was just a mite too pretty and too helpless to be left safely alone with any gentleman. And this, after all, wasn't just any gentleman. This was Roland Bentley.

"What do you suppose could be happening to cause people to disappear?" she asked after a long moment of worrying over it.

"I haven't the foggiest, but I'm not yet ready to blame a random ghost."

"Not? Even after everything we've encountered here?"

"I still maintain that there has to be some rational explanation for all of it," he said. "In fact—"

Once again, the calm was shattered by terrifying sound. This time the sound was, indeed, shattering. Somewhere nearby something had crashed loudly.

Was it a window? Had someone fallen through, or been tossed? All manner of horrible scenarios ran through Amelie's mind. She shot a quick glance up at Roland.

"I suppose there's a rational explanation for that?"

"Let's go find it," he replied.

Chapter 9

She hung just slightly behind Roland as he led the way. There were no further sounds of destruction, but Amelie couldn't quite convince herself there would not still be more. This night was proving that nothing was certain and they should all expect the unexpected.

After all, who could have ever expected that she would be huddling beside Roland now, behaving as if they were the best of friends again?

"I think it was this way," he said when they came to yet another branch off of the main corridor.

She concurred and they continued on. They hadn't gone very far when something crunched under his feet. She stepped aside and he held the lamp lower to study the floor.

"Glass," he announced.

"What kind of glass?"

She leaned in to examine it. Not window glass, so that was a good thing. Her worries for that had been unfounded. They weren't anywhere near a window, in fact. But what could have made that loud crashing sound? Certainly something much more substantial than this tiny shard.

"It appears to be from a bottle," Roland said, holding the piece up to the light. Oddly enough, he sniffed it, then pronounced, "whiskey."

"A whiskey bottle? But where is the rest of it?"

"I hate to say it, but it could be being used as a weapon. Broken glass can be quite lethal, as a matter of fact."

"Lethal? Oh heavens. Whatever could someone be up to?"

"I don't know, but I'm pretty sure a ghost wouldn't have need of a weapon."

"Then the question is, who do we know who has a proclivity for whiskey bottles?"

The answer was painfully obvious. Amelie didn't want to say it, but how could she not? She sighed. They both spoke the name together.

"Mr. Maitland."

"Poor Lady Gladbourne's father," she bemoaned. "He always smells of liquor."

"Exactly. Even in the short time I've been here, I've noted that certain air about him."

"He's such a kind gentleman, though," Amelie pointed out. "Surely he would never abduct women or terrorize his daughter this way."

"Then perhaps we ought to find him and see for ourselves just what he's up to."

"Listen! What is that?"

Her ears perked to a sound, slight and almost inaudible. It was as if someone was moving furniture, like wood scraping against wood.

"Come on," Roland whispered. "It's just around that corner."

They tiptoed around the next corner and could hear the sound louder, clearer. There was nothing to be seen, just another corridor with a series of doors. The sound, however, very clearly came from behind one of them. Roland pointed.

She nodded to assure him that she understood. They were going to go silently in the hopes of surprising their quarry. Perhaps the missing women were inside, or perhaps a villain with the jagged neck of a broken bottle. Either way, Amelie was happy to let Roland go first.

He carefully undid the latch at the door. Holding his lamp behind him so that the light did not give them away, he cracked the door just a bit. The grating sound stopped, replaced by muffled shuffling.

Roland threw the door open and charged inside. Amelie followed, determined to be useful should he need her in some way. It was obvious the moment they were inside, though, that he did not.

Aside from ghostly draped furniture, the room was empty.

"Where did he go?" she asked.

Roland spun round, letting the lamp light infiltrate every corner, every nook behind every object. He stomped to the window and pulled back the drapes; nothing but dingy panes and the cloudy night sky beyond. There was absolutely no one in the room and no other way out.

For a moment they stood there, gawking at the situation. Then things got worse. The door they had just come through slammed shut. Amelie jumped, and ran to it instinctively. It wouldn't budge.

"We've been locked in!" she cried.

Roland shook his head. "This is the damnedest house I've ever been in."

She whirled to glare at him. "*Now* will you allow that there might be a ghost?"

"No, but I think that your lover is going to want to know what you were doing locked in a secluded bedroom with me all night."

He was smiling and patted the tall, heavily draped post of the huge bed that dominated the room. Her mind finally stopped reeling enough for his words to sink in.

"My *lover*?"

*   *   *

He had to admit, he enjoyed watching the fury burst into flame in her eyes. Apparently she did not like it one bit that he had found out her secret. Especially since she'd admitted that in her panic she'd abandoned the man to some

159

super-natural fates.

Well, she was here in this room with *him*, not with Lord Larry. Like it or not, those fates favored Roland right now and Larry was left to settle for his wife.

"What do you mean, *my lover*?" she fumed.

"You didn't think I knew about that, did you?"

"I don't think *I* know about that. What are you talking about?"

"You and Lord Larry, of course."

"Me and... you are insane. What are you insinuating?"

"I'm not insinuating anything, I'm stating the fact. You were on your way to meet him last night when you walked in on me. Don't deny it."

"I *will* deny it. I was on my way to hide from a ghost!"

"Come, Amelie. A ghost?"

"I'm telling you, Roland, there was something in that hallway with me."

"So we're back to first names again."

She rolled her eyes and crossed her arms angrily in front of her. "I thought we were back to treating each other in a civilized manner, but apparently not. Why on earth would you think I might possibly be having an affair with Lord Larry?"

"I've seen you laughing with him, letting him lead you to dinner."

"He's my host, and my friend. I have known him and Lord Gladbourne most of my life. More importantly, Lord Larry is my best friend's husband! How can you possibly think there could be anything between us beyond that?"

"You're saying there isn't?"

"Of course I'm saying there isn't."

"But surely there is someone. You told Lady Gladbourne—" He stopped himself. Demme, but he'd said too much.

"You overheard my conversation with Lady Gladbourne?"

"Enough of it to know there is someone you've been rather secretive about," he replied. "So who is he? Some randy bounder not worth his salt?"

"Oh, he's a bounder, indeed. I cannot believe you would eavesdrop on such a personal conversation!"

"Can you blame me?" he said and left his post near the bed, marching across the room to her. "I came all this way, slogged through downpours and mud, all to attend this ruddy house party where I knew that you'd be, only to find that you'd gone and given your heart to some other. Dash it all, Amelie. How could I not eavesdrop on such tragic news?"

He expected more fury, but instead she tipped her head and gave him a wary smile. "You think it would be tragic if I had given my heart?"

"Yes. Beyond comprehension."

"Well then, I hate to have to inform you, but my heart has been lost for some time now."

He knew he should have expected those words, but they stung. It had been foolish of him to think he might still stand any chance, but he was never one to run from a challenge. She had every reason to forget him and transfer her affections to another. He'd simply somehow have to find a way to live with that.

"You deserve to find contentment," he said. "I'm happy for you."

"Are you? Because I'm not content with my situation at all, especially if you are so eager to match me up with someone else."

"But you said—"

"I lost my heart years and years ago, Roland Bentley. To *you*. Do you have any idea how long I waited for you to finally notice me and get around to asking me to marry you? And then you had the nerve to break it off and abandon me! Honestly, how I cannot *hate* you is beyond me."

He had to just stand there a moment and let her words sink into his brain. "You don't hate me?"

"Oh, I've tried, believe me, and at first I thought maybe I could muster up some enduring resentment, but sadly, I've failed miserably all of this time. I couldn't possibly carry on some clandestine affair with Lord Larry or any other man on the planet because none of them is you."

He stammered, looking for the right words and finally simply gave up. What good were words, anyway? He closed the gap between them and swept Amelie into his arms, holding her the way he had wanted to for so long, and begging for her forgiveness.

"It was too much scandal," he said, stroking her silky hair and pressing kisses onto her head. "My family was ruined and my father was dead. I couldn't bring you into that madness. You deserved better, Amelie. I made the decision to set you free and I thought I could live with that."

"It was a stupid decision," she murmured, snuggling against him.

"I know, and I've suffered immensely. But little by little people grew tired of vilifying my family. The scandal grew cold and now no one cares anymore. Along the way, I've made some investments and recouped some of the losses. I'm not the pariah I thought that I was, Amelie. When I learned that you'd be here, and that you were still single, I decided to accept the invitation."

"That was a much better decision."

"Agreed, despite the bedlam I find myself in just now. I love you, Miss D'Arnaud. It makes me do foolish, ridiculous things. I will battle ghosts and dark hallways or anything you ask, but please, say you will give me a second chance."

"Of course I will, Roland. I never stopped loving you. I will say, though, that if you try to back out of it this time, you will end up believing in ghosts because you will *be* one."

He had to laugh at her, despite the fact that he knew she was only half joking. "Fair enough, my love. Fair enough."

She smiled up at him and her lips were so pretty, so close to his own, that he took them with a kiss. She sighed and gave herself up to him, kissing him with the same heat, the same longing that burned within him. He was rather thrilled to be locked in this room with her. The rest of the household could go to Hades.

"Roland," she said softly, pushing him away far too soon. "Did you hear that?"

To be honest, he hadn't heard anything above the pounding of blood in his veins. But she seemed quite perplexed, so he forced himself to give up on kissing and hear her concerns.

"What is it?" he asked.

"A key just clicked in the door!"

Sure enough, he turned to the door and reached for the handle that Amelie had tried unsuccessfully just minutes ago. This time it opened right away. Demme it all, but they were no longer locked in this room. Whoever had trapped them, presumably, had come along to release them, for some reason. They'd been held here just long enough to secure their happy future.

"Footsteps," she noted.

Indeed, there were footsteps fading in the distance. Their captor was retreating! Roland grabbed up the trusty lamp and took Amelie's hand.

"Let's go end this, once and for all."

Chapter 10

They followed the footsteps around a corner and onto the landing of a great staircase. It hadn't seemed that the footsteps went down the stairs, but where else could they have gone? There was no one in sight.

"I fear that we lost him," Roland growled. "There's no other way he could have gone, yet we were close enough that we should have seen him on the staircase."

Amelie agreed. Something was clearly not right. How could their quarry have just disappeared? That seemed to be happening far too often around here. She studied the sweeping staircase and the landing where they stood.

"I think I came through here with Lord Larry and Cristina when we first began our hunt tonight," she said finally. "This was once the main part of the house, when it was originally built years and years ago.

"A fascinating history. Did Lord Larry mention how people could vanish right in front of us in his God-forsaken house?"

"No, but he did mention his early ancestors were Catholic."

"You were discussing religion with him?"

"He was keeping up conversation so Cristina and I wouldn't be scared. But you know, if there were Catholics in the house, that likely meant priests. As I recall from my schoolroom lessons, that was not well abided during certain times."

Roland's eyes narrowed and he nodded. Apparently the same notion that struck her had just become obvious to him, also.

"That could mean this house was build with a priest

hole," he said.

"Or several," she replied, already moving toward the wall at the other side of their landing.

English country halls were notorious for secret hiding places and emergency passages. Surely this section of Cliffside Manor was ancient enough to have needed such protections for any number of reasons; clashing feudal lords, religious persecution, clandestine efforts during the great civil war. If people were disappearing, unseen footsteps echoed, and Roland was right that there were no real ghosts, then clearly there was another explanation.

"Look," he said, stooping low beside the paneled wall. "Another piece of glass."

She peered over his shoulder to see. "It looks wet! Is that... blood?"

"Yes. And also... whiskey. It smells the same as the other."

"And the floor!" she cried.

Roland had set the lamp down, letting its light splay across the smooth stone floor of the landing. In the flickering glow, the wet sheen of footsteps were clearly visible. They seemed to disappear directly into the wall.

"A secret door!" she exclaimed, jumping to her feet.

In her haste, she bumped into a short decorative column that had been placed there to hold the marble bust of some ancient Garville patriarch. She grabbed for the bust to steady it, but found it was not wobbling at all. In fact, it was fixed perfectly tight to the column it sat on. Even more surprising, it was not marble, but wood, merely painted to look as marble.

"Look at this," she said. "There's something odd about his bust."

Roland rose and moved to her side. Lamplight illuminated the bust and instantly Amelie choked back a cry. A bloody red handprint covered the back of the bust's head.

While she staggered in shocked terror, Roland investigated more closely. He touched the bust, placing his own hand on the head and then, oddly enough, turning it. The head moved!

With the soft creak of a hinge, one of the wall panels suddenly swung open. This was even more shocking than the bloody handprint! So there really were secret passages in this house, and they had just found one.

Roland smiled at her. "Are you game for it?"

He expected her to climb in there after their murderous quarry? No, indeed she was *not* game for this! But the thought that Aunt Tabitha—or even Miss Fairwell, she supposed—could be somewhere hidden behind this wall, terrified and in danger, made her pluck up her courage.

"Let's go," she said boldly.

Roland smiled at her and stuck his head into the opening behind the panel. She took a deep breath, ready to follow, but suddenly he retreated. He held his fingers to his lips, warning her to be silent, and carefully shut the panel again.

"Someone's coming!" he whispered, grabbing Amelie's hand and pulling her off to the side.

They were barely out of the way when the panel slid open again and a man clad in dark clothes emerged. Good heavens, but their quarry had come to them! Amelie held her breath and hid herself as best she could behind Roland's broad figure.

The man from the secret passageway noticed the light from their lamp almost immediately. He stopped still, and he cursed. Before he could turn and disappear into the wall again, though, Roland pounced on him.

They scuffled and Amelie covered her mouth to keep from screaming like a frightened child. What if this person was armed! Oh, but he might hurt Roland, and then turn on her. She wished that silly bust wasn't affixed to its stand. It would have been perfect to grab up and then crash over their assailant's head.

But Roland had everything well in hand. Before long, the struggle ceased and he had his prey by the collar. Amelie blinked in amazement.

"Mr. Maitland!"

"We thought as much," Roland said. "You left a trail of whiskey behind, sir, while you conducted your dirty business."

"Please don't tell Mrs. Dibbley!" the man begged.

Now that statement had been unexpected.

"Er, you mean Aunt Tabitha?" Amelie asked.

"Yes," Mr. Maitlaind whined, shaking his graying head sadly. "I've tried so hard not to let her know I was drinking. I tried to quit, really I did, because I know how she feels about such things."

"She disapproves of your whiskey so you abducted and murdered her?" Amelie questioned.

"Murdered? Good heavens, no. I would never harm my Tabby. What do you mean, abducted her? By God, what has happened?"

He honestly did not seem to know. Amelie exchanged glances with Roland and he shrugged. It was beginning to seem as if they had not captured their culprit, after all.

"What is wrong with your hand, sir?" Roland asked, indicating the bloody handkerchief wrapped around one of Mr. Maitland's hands.

In his other hand he held a large sack. It rattled and tinked when he moved it.

"I cut myself on one of the bottles," the man replied. "I'd been keeping my stash hidden in odd parts of the house, hoping Tabby and my daughter wouldn't find out.

They do so much want me to stop, but it's terribly hard, you know? Well, with all of this ghost nonsense going on, I didn't know what to do so I decided to just rid myself once and for all."

"Rid yourself of what?" Roland asked him. "Your accusers? Are you so desperate to protect your sordid secret?"

"What? No, I'm desperate to be rid of the *whiskey*," Mr. Maitland replied, rattling the bag in his hand. "It's held me prisoner for so long, now it has to go. Rather than letting any of you ghost hunters stumble across it on your search tonight, I was gathering up all my bottles—every wicked drop I had hidden in this house—and I planned to dump it out a window."

It was beginning to make sense to Amelie, but Roland still eyed the man with suspicion. Clearly he needed a bit more convincing.

"If you were so worried about keeping it secret, why were you smashing your bottles where we all might hear you?"

Mr. Maitland seemed almost in a panic. "That was an accident! I had gone to retrieve the bottle I kept in that far wing, but then someone ran into me in the corridor. I don't know who, but it was dark and he was moving fast. I dropped the bottle and it shattered. Well, I knew anyone could hear, so I gathered the bits and got into one of those secret passages quick, so no one would find me. I even cut myself in my hurry."

"There was a secret passageway in that area of the house?" Roland asked.

"Oh, they are all over. The house is well riddled with them. They made it easy for me to keep up my secret trips to my stash. But no more! I'm done with the drink. I'm going to be a new man for my Tabby."

"So you're not the one who took her?" Amelie asked.

"Took her? What the devil are you talking about?"

"Mrs. Dibbley disappeared somehow tonight," Roland answered. "Miss Fairwell, too. And someone locked us in a room."

Now Mr. Maitland seemed honestly confused. Concerned, too. "Well, that's been none of my doing. Are they safe? And what of Netta, my daughter? Is she in any danger?"

They explained as much as they knew, and Mr. Maitland did, too. As best they could tell, he'd been collecting his stash in other parts of the building when the disappearances occurred. He knew nothing of the sounds they had heard that lured them into that empty bedroom, and he swore that he'd not been the one to lock them in there.

"I heard all the running, and you two chasing after someone, so I hurried in here." He pointed to the panel he had just emerged from.

"We saw your bloody handprint on the bust that triggers the opening," Roland said. "But you were safely away. Why did you return to this spot?"

Now Mr. Maitland's eyes went wide. "Because I wasn't alone in there! Someone else is using these passages tonight, and I'll bet my life he's the one who's taken our ladies!"

Chapter 11

There was obviously only one thing to do: they had to climb through that panel and go after this mysterious prowler. Amelie felt her blood run cold at the very idea of that, but Roland took her hand between both of his.

"We could simply go find the others and find a few footmen to send on this errand," he said.

Of course that was an option. It sounded like a good one, too, except that it would give their villain even more time to escape or do dastardly things to Aunt Tabitha and Miss Fairwell. Despite the dark cloud of terror looming over her now, Amelie knew there was only one thing they could do.

"Show us the way, Mr. Maitland."

He nodded, his bag of bottles rattling and dripping whiskey as he went. The man disappeared into the wall panel and Roland held up his lamp, helping Amelie to go inside next. To Amelie's surprise, there was more than just Roland's lamplight inside.

"I lit a few wall lamps," Mr. Maitland said. "So I could move about safely and find my way."

"It appears you helped our perpetrator, too," Roland noted.

"I'll make short work of him when we get him," Mr. Maitland grumbled, jostling his bag and turning sideways to move through the rough, narrow passage. "If he has in any way harmed my Tabitha..."

"Let's just focus on finding everyone unharmed," Roland said, sensibly.

Amelie let the men usher her along and she tried not to think about the cobwebs and crawling things they encountered along the way. Whoever Mr. Maitland had thought he needed to get away from was obviously nowhere near them by now, so they kept on. Finally, Mr. Maitland turned to them and whispered to stay very quiet. It seemed they had come to the end of their route.

Slowly and silently, he pulled at a knob that hung from a fraying string emerging through the wall. It must have released a latch, because the flat wall before him suddenly shifted. It made a low grating sound. Amelie realized she'd heard this sound earlier, just before they'd been locked in that room.

She glanced back at Roland and he nodded. Yes, he recognized it, too. No wonder when they went into that room they had found it empty. The sound they had heard was someone operating one of these secret panels! Their tormentor tonight had lured them there with that racket, then neatly disappeared into the wall to come around and lock them inside. It made her furious to think they had been so used, even if their time in that room had been well-spent.

She peered past Mr. Maitland as the wall opened up into a room. It was not the room they had been locked in, but it was another room where she had been. It was the room with all the doors, the one that Lord Larry claimed gave access to several areas of this end of the house, wings stemming off in different directions with corridors looping back to make just about anyone who tried to navigate it quite mad.

She shuddered to realize how near they were now to that strange room with the drapery and the gypsy runes on the table. And the hands in the dark. Gracious, how she never wanted to feel that sort of terror again!

All appeared safe now, so the stepped into the room. Roland bravely hoisted the lamp and kept Amelie securely at his side. A scan of the area showed they were alone.

That, however, did not last for long. Almost instantly the glow of another lamp spilled through one of the random doorways. It was followed by the arrival of Lord and Lady Gladbourne.

"Papa!" She exclaimed, rushing to Mr. Maitland. "We've been looking everywhere for you. Where have you been? And oh, what happened to your hand?"

The man didn't get a chance to answer. Another doorway brightened with approaching lamplight and very soon Mr. and Mrs. Garville were there. They rushed in, Cristina especially happy to see everyone.

"Here you all are! Good heavens, I keep losing everyone tonight. I even lost Lord Larry for a moment."

"You have found me now, dearest," Lord Larry said in his usual jovial tone. "But I say, what a motley crew. What has everyone been up to?"

His raised eyebrows and the teasing glance he sent specifically toward Roland and Amelie made her blush. He must have been able to sense the change in their demeanor. No doubt others would wonder about it, too. As soon as everything was sorted out and everyone in their group was safe, Amelie would take great joy in making their announcement. Hopefully her dear friends would be happy for her, despite the dislike they had expressed for poor Roland and his misguided treatment of her.

"I was worried you had been harmed," Amelie said, smiling at Cristina and truly thrilled to see her so safe and sound. "What on earth happened in that horrible room?"

Cristina simply shrugged. "I have no idea. The light went out and you screamed, the next thing I knew, I was tripping over pillows as someone very nearly trampled me. When Larry finally found the tinder to get his lamp burning again, you were gone!"

"We went to find you, and that's when we were separated," Lord Larry added. "But now you are found and

173

everyone is together again."

"Not everyone," Mr. Maitland pointed out. "Where is Mrs. Dibbley?"

Worried glances and fretful mumbling filled the room. Then the wall creaked and ground its way open once again. Aunt Tabitha stepped out.

Mr. Maitland was the only one not too amazed to speak. "Tabby? You were the one following me in the passageway?"

"I was so proud of you, Harry!" she said with a huge, happy smile. "You were gathering up all of that dreadful whiskey and I knew you were giving it up for me."

"I know how you hate it, my dear," Mr. Maitland said, moving to her. "Have I convinced you? Do you believe I can change and truly be worthy of you?"

"I do believe you, Harry, and I love you for it. But..."

Mr. Maitland looked crestfallen. "But what? You are still refusing to marry me?"

Lady Gladbourne was watching this interplay with great interest. Apparently the relationship between her father and Tabitha Dibbley was as much a surprise to her as it was to everyone else. Who could have guessed these two older people were cooing and mooning behind everyone's backs?

But there was little cooing now. Aunt Tabitha shook her head sadly as she replied.

"How can I *not* refuse you, dear Harry? You know where things stand. Until I have heard from poor Erwin, I simply can't tell you yes. It could be too dangerous."

"Dangerous?" Roland asked. Amelie very much liked that he stepped an inch or two closer to her. "What danger are you talking about?"

"From the Erwin, of course," Aunt Tabitha replied with a sigh. "We quarreled before he died... I'm afraid he had a

174

problem with his drinking, too, and he knew I disapproved of it. Oh, I said some terrible things the last time we spoke. His ghost has haunted me ever since."

"So you're saying these ghostly occurrences are really just Uncle Erwin?" Cristina questioned.

"I'm afraid so. If he is unhappy about me marrying again, there's no telling what he might do. All these years I've refused to go back to our home; his spirit terrified me so much there. I was thankful he never followed me to any of the places I've stayed."

"But if his spirit didn't follow you, how can he be haunting you here?" Amelie had to ask.

Now Aunt Tabitha gave a sheepish reply. "Because I've summoned him."

"You've summoned him?" Mr. Maitland asked.

"Yes. I wanted to explain to him about you... about us. I needed to know he would give us his blessing. You understand, Harry, don't you?"

Mr. Maitland took Aunt Tabitha's hand and patted it gently. "Of course I understand, Tabby."

Amelie wasn't sure she did, though. Those strange footsteps in the hallway, the other unexplained things they'd experienced... these were manifestations of the deceased Mr. Dibbley? How on earth did one summon a ghost? Ah, but she thought she knew. The strange things they'd discovered in that mystical room earlier suddenly made sense.

"The gypsy runes, and the crystal ball!" she exclaimed. "Those are yours, Aunt Tabitha, aren't they? You were trying to make some sort of magic to summon your husband."

"That's right," Aunt Tabitha admitted. "And I'm sorry I frightened you. You see, my group was searching the house and we heard some other-worldly sounds. I just knew it was poor Erwin, so I left my group and hurried back to that secret room. When your group found it, I hid behind the drapery. But then you took up the brooch and, well, I couldn't let you compromise it."

"The brooch that you said you mislaid?" Cristina interrupted.

"Yes, that one. I didn't want to admit where it was, that I was using it for a talisman in my séances. The spirits are very particular about those things, you see, and if I hoped to summon Erwin, I needed a beloved object that held powerful energies. If Miss D'Arnaud tainted it, that might ruin everything."

"So you attacked me in the dark?" Amelie asked.

"Heavens no! At least, not on purpose. I didn't mean to put the light out, but when I flung back the drapery I was hiding behind, I suppose I caused a draft and blew out the light. And then as I was fumbling around, I nearly fell over you. I hope I didn't hurt you, my dear."

"No, I just... I'm sorry that I became so upset."

So those had been Aunt Tabitha's hands in the dark, grabbing for her? Clearly Amelie over-reacted. Perhaps her imagination had run away with her and not let her realize what truly was happening. She'd struggled and screamed, and run away before the old woman had a chance to explain. No doubt Amelie's distress had caused Lord Larry and Cristina to be flustered and fearful, as well.

"So what you are saying," Roland noted as they all digested these new revelations. "Is that there really is no ghost at all. We have an explanation for nearly everything."

Aunt Tabitha frowned. "What do you mean?"

"Well, we've uncovered the source of those footsteps and bumps in the night; they were just Mr. Maitland using secret passageways to tend his secret cache."

The gentleman in question shrugged in acknowledgement. "It's true; I am guilty. But never again, I swear it."

"Good for you, sir," Roland continued. "We have explanation for the shattered glass, for Miss D'Arnaud's screams, and for Aunt Tabitha's disappearance. What I still cannot understand—and I'm finding it hard to credit to a ghost—is who took Miss Fairwell?"

Aunt Tabitha seemed honestly amazed. "Miss Fairwell is missing?"

Chapter 12

Roland waited for a sensible answer. Everyone in the room stared at one another, glancing around, hoping someone could explain. Fear in the air was becoming thick as one by realization showed on their faces. Either there really was a ghost in the house, or there was a possible murderer!

Tension was high and the silence was ominous. Finally, someone took credit.

"Oh, very well. I did it!"

Roland's eyebrows rose dramatically. Along with everyone else, he turned to the speaker. *Impossible.* There had to be some explanation to follow.

"Lord Larry?" Amelie gasped.

"Yes, yes. I took her," their host announced. "But not for any nefarious purpose. She's just fine. I put her in Aunt Tabitha's room back there and told her we were pulling a prank, playing a joke on everyone."

His wife smacked him on the arm. "You kidnapped Miss Fairwell? What's wrong with you!"

"Nothing. Ouch." Lord Larry rubbed his arm and moved just out of her reach. "I knew we needed to do something about Miss D'Arnaud and Roland, so I got Miss Fairwell out of the way."

"What?!" His wife smacked him again.

Roland was beginning to wonder if matrimony wasn't a more dangerous institution than he'd anticipated.

"That's why I locked them in that bedroom," Lord Larry added.

"Bedroom?!!" his wife cried. Roland though she might be going to strangle him this time.

179

"You're the one who locked us in there?" Amelie asked. "Why on earth would you do that?"

Lord Larry had a ready reply. "It was obvious the two of you have been carrying a torch all this time. I knew that all you needed was some enforced time alone to engage in meaningful conversation—or something—to iron out your differences."

"But you locked us in a room!" Amelie reiterated.

"And then I let you out," Larry replied, giving Roland a sly smile. "I believe things worked themselves out in the end, didn't they?"

Roland had to acquiesce. "Well done, my friend. I suppose I owe you."

"You mean... things are settled between you?" Cristina questioned, gaping incredulously at Amelie.

Roland found it more than a little gratifying to know that the rosy flush in Amelie's cheeks was due in great part to her recollections of their time locked in that room. She nodded modestly and smiled a prim smile.

"Yes, very much so," she said. "We have, as Lord Larry said, ironed out some differences."

The ladies in the room all tittered.

"Well then," Lord Larry declared. "I guess there is no need to keep Miss Fairwell penned up in that creepy séance room, is there?"

His wife smacked him again for good measure. "Certainly not. Let's get her immediately."

*   *   *

The whole group traipsed out of the room, through one of the doorways, and up a narrow corridor. They had enough lamps between them to make the place quite bright, and honestly it was almost inviting. Amelie still shuddered as she recalled her previous horror as she ran through this passage earlier, stumbling in darkness and convinced that an evil specter was reaching out for her from beyond the grave.

How nice to know it was really only Aunt Tabitha falling on top of her.

"Here we go," Lord Larry said as they came to the doorway to the little room.

He pushed the door open and stepped inside. Amelie was just close enough to see past him. Sure enough, Miss Fairwell was alive and well, nestled quite comfortably among the many pillows. She stirred, blinked her blue eyes, and gave a little yawn.

"Oh, here you are," she said cordially. "Is the joke over? Did we make everyone wonder where I had gone?"

"Yes," Lord Larry replied. "Everyone certainly wondered."

Cristina poked him and he winced. "Now tell her you are sorry for leaving her here all alone. Honestly, what could you be thinking? Look at this place. She was probably terrified!"

But Miss Fairwell merely sat up quite properly and smiled at them. "Oh no, I wasn't frightened at all. Lord Larry left his uncle to look after me."

"See?" Lord Larry said, obviously pleased that his wife should get such a glowing report. Then his face fell. "Er, what's that about my uncle?"

"That kind old man who was with me," Miss Fairwell said. "He was so gentle and sweet. He said he was your uncle and that he was very proud of you. He thinks you've done remarkably well with your choice of wife."

"Yes, of course, but—"

"What else did this wise old man say to you?" Cristina questioned.

Miss Fairwell screwed up her face as she tried to recall. Even that did not make her look anything but lovely.

Amelie hoped that Roland might not notice.

A secret glance up at him, thankfully, confirmed that his gaze was only for her.

"He told me that he's been worried for Aunt Tabitha, but he wants me to give her a message," Miss Fairwell said slowly. "Let's see if I can get it right... he said she should be very happy with someone hairy?"

"With someone *named* Harry?" Aunt Tabitha asked quickly.

"Yes, that sounds right," Miss Fairwell replied, and then laughed. "Whoever Harry is, he's not a drunk and that's a good thing, I suppose. Oh, and something silly, too. Lord Larry's uncle said that your house is haunted, Aunt Tabitha. He told me you might not want to go back there. Those ghosts aren't very nice."

Aunt Tabitha made an odd squeaking sound, so Mr. Maitland put his arm around her. Amelie wondered if perhaps this was another of Lord Larry's machinations, but one look at him dispelled that suspicion. His face was as ashen as everyone else's.

Cristina was looking around the room. "Where is this gentleman now?"

"He must have left," Miss Fairwell answered. "When we got done playing with those funny stones on the table, he said it was time for him to go. I'm afraid I felt drowsy so I must have dozed off."

"You were playing with the stones on the table?" Amelie asked. Sure enough, she could tell the gypsy runes had been rearranged completely.

"He said they are some kind of fortune telling tool," Miss Fairwell said with a perky nod. "So, he laid them out and he told me my fortune."

"And what is your fortune?" Lord Larry asked.

Now Miss Fairwell giggled. "I'm going to meet a tall,

dark stranger and fall hopelessly in love. Isn't that wonderful?"

There were murmurs all around. Amelie slipped her hand through Roland's arm and held on tightly. Miss Fairwell didn't care. She smiled benignly and seemed utterly clueless to what had been transpiring all night.

"Well, what do you know," Roland said. He had pulled his watch from his pocket and was studying it. "It's only just midnight. It would appear the truth has come out for all of us."

"Exactly as the tea leaves said," Aunt Tabitha breathed.

"Well then," Lord Gladbourne said, clearing his throat. "I believe we are done here. I, myself, plan to go to bed and forget any of this ever happened."

"Well, the scary parts, at least," Lady Gladbourne agreed.

The group shuffled from the room, Cristina ushering Miss Fairwell along and giving Lord Larry a look that said there'd be discussion to follow. Amelie was glad to leave that room with its odd implements behind. It would be good to be back in the more familiar parts of the house.

"I think I'll be sleeping with a light tonight," Lady Gladbourne said.

"Two of them," Amelie amended. "I'll probably jump at every sound until sunrise."

"Why?" Miss Fairwell asked. "Why is everyone acting so frightened?"

"Because, Poppy," Cristina said sweetly. "My husband doesn't have an uncle of that description. Not since Erwin Dibbley died fifteen years ago."

Chapter 13

They were back in the warmer, brighter, friendlier part of the house. Amelie was wondering how she would subtly find a few moments alone again with Roland. It was doubtful she'd be so fortunate as to accidentally walk in on him again, but she hoped that at least they could find a few moments in a dark corner to say their good-nights. Netta and Cristina were watching her like hawks, though, so it was going to be tricky.

It would be especially hard to find a dark corner, too. Even at midnight the servants in the is part of the house were still bustling, the lights all still burning. There was quite a commotion, actually.

The housekeeper rushed up to Cristina to explain. "We have more guests, ma'am. They only just arrived."

"Who is it?" Cristina asked.

"Your parents, and a friend of theirs," the housekeeper replied.

Cristina beamed with excitement. "How wonderful! I was hoping they could make it."

Their group was just coming into the grand entrance hall. Servants scurried past as the trio of new arrivals huddled there removing coats and unloading bags that seemed to indicate they intended to stay for a while. Lord Larry seemed just a bit dubious at the loads of luggage, but Cristina clearly rejoiced.

She gathered her group of guests together to make introductions. Amelie felt woefully self-conscious. Oh, but she could only imagine how she must look—cobwebs in her hair, dust on her gown, who knew what on her slippers—but she supposed the rest of her friends did not look much better. Hopefully Cristina's parents would be too tired to noticed their bedraggled state.

She felt especially drab when introduced to the visitor who accompanied Cristina's parents. He was a tall man with chiseled features and a deep, dusky Spanish accent. Lord Larry was noticeably cool toward him and begrudgingly introduced the man as Don Bernardo Miguel Garcia de la Vaca. It was quite an auspicious name, to be sure, but he was gracious and friendly, pausing over each lady's hand to utter some bit of flattery and small talk. Until he was introduced to Miss Fairwell.

The look that passed between these two strangers was more than compelling. Amelie couldn't help but stare. For the first time ever, Miss Fairwell seemed at a loss for words. Don Bernardo, as well. Several seconds passed while those two stood, their eyes locked in some sort of unexplained communion. Amelie knew what was happening, of course.

She probably had the same star-struck look on her face every time that she looked at Roland. He must have seen it, too, for he leaned close to her. His voice rumbled with mirth and affection as he whispered into her ear.

"I will never discount tea leaves again."

"It is a remarkable coincidence," Amelie asserted. "She's met a tall, dark stranger and they are instantly in love! Just as the tea leaves and the gypsy runes predicted."

"Well then, perhaps I have something to hope for tonight."

"Oh? Was there a prediction for you?"

"No, but if the spirits can tell our futures, then perhaps they will haunt the halls again tonight. With any luck, they might chase you into my room."

She blushed involuntarily. "Oh no, I won't leave the safety of my locked door tonight. If you expect me to darken your threshold again, sir, you'll have to make it all the way to the altar."

Roland didn't seem too much put off. He slipped his hand into hers, lacing their fingers and apparently not caring what others around them might think.

"No ghost or ghoul could keep me from it," he promised. "I *will* marry you, Amelie, and I'll love you every day of this life."

"And in the afterlife?" she asked him.

"Then I will haunt you, my dearest."

Other Regency Romance by Susan Gee Heino

The Earl's Passionate Plot
The Earl's Intimate Error
The Earl's Christmas Delivery
Miss Farrow's Feathers
Miss Wheaton's Whiskers
Yuletide Lies
Passion and Pretense
Temptress in Training
Damsel in Disguise
Mistress by Mistake

Note from the Author:

I truly hope you have enjoyed these tales of Lord Larry. I've really enjoyed crafting them.

Lord Larry made his first appearance in "The Delicate Plot to Bury Lord Larry," *a short story that was originally published in the anthology,* "Fifty Ways to Kill Your Larry." *Ten authors participated in that project, and the point was for each of us to write a short story in which our individually created Larry would die. It could be a real death, a perceived death, or a metaphorical death. I chose an intentionally staged death for my Larry.*
(You can find out more about these stories at **www.RedDoorReads.com***.)*

But Larry was a lovable character and I knew he needed to find some happiness for himself. So, I wrote "The Elegant Scheme to Marry Lord Larry" *followed up by* "The Ghostly Goal of Scary Lord Larry". *Thank you for joining Larry on his journey. We've seen him lose love, find it again, and now he's helped others to gain their happily-ever-afters, too. In a roundabout way, of course. That's just how Larry rolls and I simply can't help but love him for it.*

I write romance because there's always a happy ending. In real life, things don't often go as planned, so I try to give readers a few pages of blissful escape and, hopefully, a few smiles. Because, you know, love's funny sometimes!

About the Author

Susan Gee Heino thinks the sexiest thing a man can do is engage in witty banter. If he happens to be wearing breeches and a cravat while he does this, all the better. If he comes with a noble title, a tortured past, and perhaps even dimples, then he is just about perfect.

Her lighthearted Regency Romances are full of quirky heroines who tend to feel exactly the same way—at least they do by the end of the book. Usually it takes a little convincing by the cravat-clad hero. But no matter what adventures ensue, the hero always ends up with his lady. And vice versa.

Ms. Heino lives in rural Ohio with her non-cravat-inclined husband, two very remarkable children, and an accidental collection of critters. She loves to hear from readers so please visit her website or connect on social media!

www. SusanGH.com
Love's funny sometimes!

195

www.ingramcontent.com/pod-product-compliance
Lightning Source LLC
Chambersburg PA
CBHW061159170626
46809CB00003B/1162